James F. B. Tinling

Early Roman Catholic Missions To India

with sketches of Jesuitism, Hindu philosophy and the Christianity of the

ancient Indo-Syrian church of Malabar - An historical essay

James F. B. Tinling

Early Roman Catholic Missions To India
with sketches of Jesuitism, Hindu philosophy and the Christianity of the ancient
Indo-Syrian church of Malabar - An historical essay

ISBN/EAN: 9783337247249

Printed in Europe, USA, Canada, Australia, Japan

Cover: Foto ©Andreas Hilbeck / pixelio.de

More available books at **www.hansebooks.com**

EARLY

ROMAN - CATHOLIC

MISSIONS TO INDIA;

WITH

SKETCHES OF JESUITISM, HINDU PHILOSOPHY,

AND

THE CHRISTIANITY OF THE ANCIENT INDO-SYRIAN

CHURCH OF MALABAR.

An Historical Essay,

BY

JAMES F. B. TINLING, B.A.,

Author of "An Evangelist's Tour Round India,"
"An Echo of the Voice of George Fox," &c.

LONDON: S. W. PARTRIDGE AND CO.,
9, PATERNOSTER ROW.
BRISTOL: W. MACK, 38, PARK STREET.
——
1871.

PREFACE.

It is particularly important in the present day to understand the true character of Roman Catholicism. Every one knows that that system has had much to do with the world's past, but there are many who think it is becoming effete, and that it will have little to do with the future. Nothing will serve better than such a belief to lead it back again to power. Without saying that it is exclusively "the mystery of iniquity," of which Paul warned the Thessalonian Christians, we believe that it is the greatest illustration of that mystery, and that it will have much to do, at least as a source or cause, with that final development of Anti-christianity which is to characterize the end of the present age, according to the Scriptures. Indeed, the variety of appearances which it has presented to the world confirms its title to the name of "mystery." Its portrait in the fifteenth century, with the gross features of immorality and ignorance, would not be recognised in the succeeding generation of the mighty Jesuits; while these again, in their day of youthful power, seem no fit representatives of the enfeebled popery of our own rationalistic age.

But the principles of the great Apostate Church are all unchanged; her claims are the same to-day as ever, and her desire and hope of enslaving the world. Her doctrines have increased, but they have not altered, so that the causes of past atrocities are still integral parts of her system, only waiting for opportunity to bear again the same black fruit. It is true that history reproduces itself, but history is made by men, and in proportion as men understand the past, they will save themselves from the reproduction of its evil.

The example which India affords of the character of Romanism is a remarkable one. Far removed from Europe and from the battle-field of the Reformation, burning with the zeal of Xavier, mighty with the swords of Portugal and the Inquisition, learned with the new-born literature of the West, and crafty with the super-human subtlety of De Nobili and Beschi, the Church of Rome exhibited in vivid colours its character, purpose, and religious ability in the early missions to India. It did battle with Brahminism on the one hand, and on the other with the ancient Christianity of Malabar; and each of these antagonists, as it came in contact with Romanism, drew out some peculiarities of the system of which, perhaps, nowhere else could we find better illustrations.

But the interest of this page of history is by no means exclusively connected with the study of Romish Christianity. The political condition of India, the land of wealth and wonder to the West, when Europeans first settled on its shores, and an Eastern Cæsar at Delhi was still claiming the allegiance of hundreds of tributary kings; the hoary philosophy of Hinduism, with its superstructure of childish polytheism, and the isolated Christian Church at Malabar, with its eight hundred years of Indian history, and its faint but most interesting testimony of spiritual truth, will, we hope, be matters of thought sufficiently interesting to commend the subject of the following essay to intelligent Christian readers. In the collection of materials the writer has freely availed himself of Hough's elaborate "History of Christianity in India," especially for the story of the Syrian Church, Steinmetz' "History of the Jesuits," Dr. Duff's "India, and Indian Missions," and Marshman's "History of India."

BRISTOL, *July,* 1871.

CONTENTS.

EARLY ROMAN-CATHOLIC MISSIONS
TO INDIA, &c.

THE present condition of India is one which makes the study of her history peculiarly interesting: it presents a contrast to every phase through which she has passed in the long ages which tell of her greatness. For more than twenty five centuries she has acted an important part in the history of the world. No country, in ancient or modern times, has, in a similar way and to the same extent, influenced the destinies of Asia and Europe: none, without a voice in the councils of civilized nations, has ever gained or been worthy of so much attention.

Introduction respecting the present condition of India —commercially —politically —religiously.

The trade with which she has enriched the kingdoms that have trafficked with her, and the almost equally continuous spoliations she has been able to endure at the hand of ruthless invaders, alike bear witness to her wealth; and to this day the rule holds good, which history has established by many examples, that the nation which draws most upon the resources of India, is at least one of the foremost nations of the world.

The story of India's foreign commerce would begin long before the reign of Sesostris in Egypt. It would follow the course of the wandering Phœnicians, and cull from the histories of Judæa and Macedon, Persia and Rome. It would lay before us the development of

Glance at the history of Indian commerce.

Europe in its merchant navies and its domestic refine-
ment, and account, in a great measure, for the rise and
fall of cities and countries; for the successive glories of
Genoa and Venice, of Portugal and Holland, and, lastly,
of Britain. It might be illustrated by the desert wonders
of Palmyra, and the busy mart of Alexander's city,
created for the transit of India's riches; and it would
end with the record of accomplished peace and union in
connection with that island of the far west, which, in
spite of its littleness, God has made able to govern the
tribes, and to absorb the commerce of the empire of
Akbar and Aurungzebe.

To the same peaceful end comes down **Past wars and**
the long story of the wars of India. Her **present peace.**
northern plain has been the world's greatest battle-field.
Persians, and Greeks, and hordes of Eastern Asia,
followed by tribe after tribe of fierce Mahometans, have
rolled over it like the fire over the prairie. Unceasing
wars within kept the cup of misery ever full; while the
establishment of Europeans on her coasts brought for a
long time only an increase of strife. But now this
afflicted country has entered on an age of peace; and
whether, by God's mercy, that peace remain unbroken
under the strong hand that preserves it, until India can
stand alone among civilized nations, or it be but a long
breathing time before further conflict, it is interesting to
look back from such an era to the different events of
earlier history, to see how some of them—even of the
darkest—were preparing the way for the present happiness, and to learn something more of the character of
man in the excitement and temptation and opportunity
of those evil times, and of the design and working of the
unknown God whose hand was ever over all.

But apart from the fact that India is **The present**
now united and at peace, and that her **phase of**
commerce, no longer partial and uncertain, **religion.**
flows in one broad and unceasing stream, the peculiarity
of her present religious state is alone of sufficient im-

portance greatly to enhance the interest of any historical events which have helped to bring it about. While furious invasions and internal wars have levelled in turns her hundreds of thrones, the huge religious system of India—the empire of the Brahmins—has survived them all. Mahometanism and Buddhism have given it the rudest shocks; but it flourished green as ever while the last Mahometan dynasty faded away, and it rolled back the tide of Buddhism from Ceylon to the borders of China.

But what neither Mahomet's generals nor Gavtama Buddha could do is being done by another power. The hand that drove aside the clouds of Europe in the sixteenth century, and took the fetters off the prisoners of darkness, is doing the same for India three centuries later. Millions of Hindus are slowly but surely passing into liberty from a despotism more searching than that of Peruvian Incas, and as tyrannical as that of mediæval Rome. The intellectually leading class of India has boldly seceded from idolatry. It is numbered already by tens of thousands, and every year increases its strength. Apart from missionary schools, with their directly Christian influence and real converts to the truth, the Government colleges of British India, and even the Hindu college itself, founded by zealous Hindus for the support of the decaying faith, are sapping the foundations of Brahminism. Each of the three Presidencies has now its university: that of Calcutta alone has received 1350 candidates for matriculation in one term; while, at the same time, nearly 500 applied for admission at Bombay. These men continually swell the ranks of the "Reformers," and strengthen one another in infidelity and deism. The boldest or most sanguine among them are not satisfied with holding the new opinions themselves. At the risk and cost of what they once held dearer than life they have become apostles of the "Indian Reformation." Their voices shake the great temples as they cry for the regeneration of their country, and thousands are convinced by their words or overcome by their enthusiasm who have not· yet dared to follow their example. Nothing can save Brahminism but power to persecute its heretics to the death. Whether this means would restore the kingdom of darkness or not we cannot say; the history of reformation in Europe affording examples both of its success and failure—in Italy, France, and Spain, on the one hand; and in Britain, Holland, and Germany, on the other. These men have as yet rather the cause of Erasmus than of Luther;. but if British power is to continue paramount in India, the era which has commenced must go on; knowledge must spread and superstition retreat before it, and the end of that which is begun must be the utter destruction of Brahminism, and the enthroning of nominal Christianity, ·or more likely of modern religious thought in its place.

Progress in every part of national education keeps pace with this great movement. Intelligent natives congregate *Progress in general knowledge.* at agricultural exhibitions, to examine, and put in use, the steam ploughs of Birmingham. Brahmins, of rigid type, travel with Sudras and Pariahs on the British railways. The Country is being welded together, not only by rail and telegraph, but by the new language which is everywhere necessary to promotion. The Bengalee reformer visits Bombay and Madras, and preaches fluently and intelligibly to those who know nothing of his native tongue. The many tribes of Bombay with their different dialects have a ready escape from Babel in the culture of this language of the far West: while the government, and merchant offices, and banks throughout the entire country are filled by these English-speaking men of every Hindu race, many of them deprived by universal peace, or by the remodelling of the Sepoy army of all prospect of honour and wealth by war, or suffering from the destruction of the native aristocracy by Lord Dalhousie's laws of "Settlement" and "Resumption."

These are the representative men of modern India.
Naturalized to their new position and life; strong and
confident; half English in manners, and perhaps in heart,
they are abolishing caste, and idolatry, and ignorance,
and closing with a growing twilight, the long night of
Brahminism. It is from this early morning of New
India that we would look back upon one of her hours of
darkness; and, if we are heart-sick at the scenes of
violence, cruelty, and fraud, and of the *Interest which
the foregoing considerations lend to Early History.*
wickedness of Pagans outdone in the name
of Jesus Christ, we have at least the
comfort of knowing that this dark hour
ushered in the dawning, and of. tracing
some connection between the tyranny and selfishness of
man, and the present deliverance which is being wrought
by the hand of God.

The Portuguese expedition to India was *Efforts to discover a new way
to India, and the
first voyage
thither by the
Cape of Good
Hope.*
the opening of intercourse between that
country and Europe by the great ocean
highway. As we have already noticed,
India was far from being an unknown land
to the people of the West for centuries
before that time. Since the Crusades had introduced
the inhabitants of Europe to the luxuries of the East,
an intense desire for trade with India had possessed
them, and the energy of cities, and of the merchant class,
which the same chivalrous wars had been the great
means of creating, was turned into this channel. But
the streams of traffic were scanty and uncertain; and,
as they flowed through Alexandria, St. Jean d'Acre and
Constantinople, the nations which possessed no influence
over these places could do little more than watch with
jealous eyes the growing wealth and power of their
fortunate neighbours. Moreover the Mahometans com-
manded the whole of the country through which Indian
merchandise had to pass on its way to Europe; and this
stimulated the efforts of Spain, Portugal, and Britain to
find some new and open route to the land of. desire.

Fleets were despatched in all directions, and, while one course conducted Columbus to the continent of America and gave Spain a richer possession than that she was looking for, the real object of search was attained by Portugal, whose Admiral, Vasco de Gama, cast anchor in the roads of Calicut, in May, 1497.

Before following the course of the history further, let us consider the importance of this arrival. It was no less than a new invasion of India; nay, it was more important than any previous invasion. There

Importance of the discovery of the sea-passage to India.

was probably nothing very formidable in the appearance of the few ships that anchored off Calicut—nothing to inspire terror like the swarms of a Tartar or Mogul Conqueror; but it was the invasion of India by Western Europe—by those hardy and enterprising nations whose warriors had conquered the conquerors of Asia, and which still were characterized by the spirit of chivalry, and by the skill and courage of the crusaders. Moreover, it was the opening of a new entrance, or rather of many such, into the heart of India. Hitherto all invaders had entered by the north-west corner, by the gates of Affghanistan. History has taught us how those gates might be locked against an enemy, so as to be more effectual than Thermopylœ was to Greece. But, even if India had learned so to use them, it was now too late; every port and roadstead on her coasts was thrown open to nations more powerful and persevering than those which had set up the successive thrones of Delhi. From this point there has been no going back, no moment when India has been free from the presence of the new invaders. The few Portuguese who accompanied Vasco de Gama were the advance guard of European armies, which, though they have wasted their strength in warring with one another, have moved on, at least as much of necessity as of choice, subduing Hindus and Mahometans alike, and merging all in the great new empire which exhibits the union of Europe and Asia. If we say that

the progress of these armies was the progress of
civilization, we must be understood to have the end
distinctly in view. The triumph of Europe is the triumph
of civilization ; yet the dealings of Europe with India
have often been more worthy of Tartars than nominal
Christians, and have disgraced in turn almost every nation
which has had a share in them.

A view of the political state of India on **The political
state of India
at the beginning
of the
16th century.** the arrival of the Portuguese is necessary
to an understanding of the history of their
colony. It was 500 years since the first
Mahometan invasion, and 1200 years since
Mahomet Ghore founded the first Mahometan empire
in India. Invasion, murder, and insurrection had
changed the dynasty many times; and when the first
Portuguese fleet arrived, the second house of Ghore was
falling to the ground. Within thirty years, and while
the new comers were still struggling for a foothold of
the soil, Baber founded the dynasty of the Moguls. The
Deccan, or India south of the Nerbudda, was long
independent of the Mahometan power. Indeed, it might
have conduced to its happiness if it had been otherwise,
for independence meant war—continual war, with all
possible sufferings and barbarities. But the sovereigns
of the Ghiljie family, the most short-lived of Indian
dynasties, carried the Mahometan arms, in the beginning
of the fourteeneth century, to Cape Comorin and subdued
the whole country, excepting the tract of land between
the Western Ghauts and the sea, which remained unmolested for some time longer.

Conquest would have been a boon, if it had been
followed by strong government, but this was not the
rule in India; the madness or incapacity of one ruler
neutralized the successes of another. The Deccan
revolted from under the monster, Mahomet Toghluk.
Two fugitives created in the extreme south the great
Hindu kingdom of Bisnaghur. When the Portuguese
arrived, the head of this kingdom reigned from sea to

sea over all the Hindus south of the river Krishna, and
counted fifty-six kings among his dependents. North
of his territory lay the Bahminy kingdom, the Mahometan
rival and oppressor of Bisnaghur, which owed its
existence to the same cause, and dated it from the same
period. It broke up at the beginning of the sixteenth
century, and gave rise to five separate Mahometan states,
of which the three most important and longest-lived
were Beejapore, Ahmednuggur, and Golconda. Anti-
cipating the history a little, we may notice here that
half a century later (1565 A.D.) these Mahometan States
united against the great rajah of the south, and utterly
destroyed the Hindu power of the Deccan in the battle
of Tellicotta, making Mahometan authority as complete
on the southern as it was on the northern side of the
Nerbudda.

The strip of country known as Malabar
had a more distinct history of its own than   History of
any other part of India. Its great inland   Malabar.
boundary—the Western Ghauts—was a wall of defence
to the people of this region when the Mahometan
armies poured down upon the Deccan, or the hostile
rajahs wasted the rest of the Peninsula with fire and
sword in their yearly wars. Almost unmolested by the
Hindu powers of the South, Malabar seems long to have
enjoyed an immunity from Mahometan invasion; but
the last great general of the Bahminy kingdom,—whose
death was the signal of its dissolution,—overran both the
Ghauts and the sea-board, and took possession of Goa, a
short time before its occupation by the Portuguese.
Native traditions assert, with a good deal of probability
from the geographical and geological character of the
district, that the whole plain of Malabar was given up
by the sea about 2,300 years ago. With the history of
its settlement in those far-off times we have nothing to
do, nor would it be possible to get any certain infor-
mation. It appears, however, that, early in the ninth
century of our era, the first independent king reigned in

Malabar, and his character and doings were of very great importance to a colony of strangers who were settled in his kingdom. These strangers were the Christians of the Syrian Church.

Of all the wonders which astonished the Portuguese on their arrival in India—and they were many,—none would be more unexpected than a Christian church or nation. The pretensions and the power of Rome during the middle ages were so prodigious, that, even now, they almost make us overlook the existence of many independent churches in different parts of the east, so that it is no wonder if the ignorant soldiers and monks of Portugal were astonished, in the first place at the profession of Christianity of the Syrians, and in the second place at their independence of Rome. Yet in truth many such churches were scattered over Asia from Mount Lebanon to India and even China, while others had long existed in Africa on the banks of the Nile.

The Syrian Church of Malabar.

Rome had not failed to labour long before this time for the conversion or rather annexation of these bodies of Christians; but she had met with little success, except where her patronage was considered sufficiently important to be bought at the expense of liberty. None of these churches was more interesting in its position and character than that of Malabar. In the land of Hindu idolatry, surrounded on all sides by the votaries of Shiva and Vishnu; in the land of yearly war and perpetual change, was settled, in peace and worldly prosperity, one of the oldest of the churches of Christendom. On the slopes of the Western Ghauts and in the plain below, were thousands of professing Christians living, and maintaining, in much of its original purity, the truth which had been entrusted to their ancestors thirteen centuries before. Although probably unknown at this time to the Mahometans, whose rapid raid from the Bahminy kingdom is not likely to have touched these settlers in the Southern end of the Serra and of

the Concan, and although exercising little of the influence
of a Missionary Church, they were nevertheless an important political power on the coast when the Portuguese
arrived in India. Their military force consisted of
40,000 well armed and disciplined soldiers, superior to
those of most native princes, while the social standing
·which they had acquired was that of equality with
the naires or nobles of Malabar.. This military
strength and political importance was the result of
the patronage of Ceram Peroumal—the sovereign
whom we have mentioned as reigning in Malabar,
nearly seven centuries before. But the foundation
of the Indian church dates much further
back than the earliest kings of Malabar. **Early evangeli-**
Lovers of tradition ascribe the first Christian **sation of India.**
labours in India to the Apostles Thomas and Bartholomew,
or to Philip's Ethiopian convert. There is neither proof
nor probability to support these assertions, but we have
some interesting fragments of history without them.
However, the gospel was carried to India, it had taken
root there before the end of the second century; for at
that date Pantænus, the head of the Catechetical School
at Alexandria, undertook a missionary journey to India
in consequence of a request for help from   **And ancient**
certain Christians who were there to **history of the**
Dionysius, the bishop of Alexandria. This **Syrian church.**
request seems to point to the probable source from
whence the Indian Christians had received their first
knowledge. No further notice of the Indian church
occurs in history (excepting the title with which an
Eastern bishop subscribed at the Council of Nice), till
the middle of the fourth century, when we are told an
interesting story of two young Christians from Tyre who
visited the Malabar coast as travellers in the company
of an elder relative, and who were retained as slaves
after the latter had been put to death. They are said to
have risen to the responsible position of regents of the
country and guardians of a young king, and to have used

their influence with great effect for the furtherance of Christianity. The elder was afterwards ordained bishop of the country by Athanasius, and became the means of converting many of the heathen to Christ. Cosmas, "the Indian voyager," in the sixth century, reported, from his own experience, the existence of Christian churches both in Ceylon and on the Western Coast, and spoke of them as Nestorians. They changed their views for those of the Jacobites in the ninth or tenth century, after the example of their patriarch at Seleucia, when the patronage of the Mahometans made the latter sect, with the Melchites, the most powerful among the churches of the East. All these churches had lost the spirit of General declension of the Eastern Churches. primitive Christianity long before this time, and in 650 A.D., a Christian writer named Jesuyab, lamenting this fact with regard to Persia and India, attributed it to the misconduct of their patriarch, the metropolitan of Persia. But such a temporary and merely governmental evil could not account for a wide-spread spiritual degeneracy. It would have been strange, indeed, if the East had been entirely unleavened by those pernicious principles which so rapidly corrupted the churches of the West. Rome in the seventh century was already far on her way to "that bad eminence" of apostacy on which she has now been seated for a thousand years. The independent churches of Europe were falling before her—Britain, France and Spain, in turn, submitting to the yoke. And the churches of Asia would have been as welcome slaves, and would, in all probability, have shared Mahometanism a wall of protection to the Indian Church. their fate, had not God cast up a barrier for their protection, which for centuries the emissaries, and even the armies of the Pope were unable to pass. That barrier was the power of the Mahometans. The presumption and fanaticism of the false prophet were overruled by the Divine hand, to be the means of keeping back the flood of apostate Christianity

from the shores of India. And during those centuries
the Syrian church had its full day of opportunity and
trial; and if, at the end of that time, it was weighed in
the balances and found wanting, it is nothing strange
that it should have been given, for a time, into the hand
of spoilers. Under the Mahometans, Christianity, such
as it was in the seventh and following centuries, spread
considerably in Asia; the conquerors for a long time
judging it good policy to patronise the followers of
Christ; and the Malabar Christians probably increased in
numbers. But the greatest cause of their Settlement of
increase, was the settlement among them, Thomas Cana, in
about the year 800 A.D., of an Armenian Malabar.
merchant, named Thomas Cana. He was possessed of
immense wealth and consequent influence. He had
two houses, one in the South, and another in
the North of Malabar, and two wives, either at
the same time or, as history by its vagueness
allows us to hope, in succession. A numerous family
by each of his wives succeeded him in the possession of
his estates; that in the south, whose head quarters were
at Cranganore, being deemed the more respectable branch,
and declining all equal intercourse with their half-
brethren of Angamale and its neighbourhood. It was
about the time of Thomas Cana's residence in the
country, and no doubt through his influence, that the
Syrians of Malabar received the privileges, which we
have already referred to, from king Ceram Peroumal.
They were a large and important class in the population
of his newly-founded kingdom, and he secured their
attachment by a wise and liberal patronage. The
Christians of the opposite coast had been persecuted by
the native princes, and had fled to the mountains; the
generosity of the new king of Malabar Christians
drew them down to his standard, and drawn together
settled them in the districts of Travancore into one
and Cochin. In civil as well as in eccle- district.
siastical matters the Syrian Church was made independent

of its Hindu rulers, and responsible to its bishops alone ;
and the precious privileges which this exceptionally
enlightened king had granted were confirmed on tablets
of brass, which the Syrians preserved till the arrival of
the Portuguese, and which still remain in existence.　In
spiritual life and in numbers they received valuable
help a century later from the visit of two missionary
ecclesiastics from Babylon, who seem to have stimulated
the church, and converted many of the heathen by
powerful preaching and a godly life.　From the measure
of prosperity they received from Ceram Peroumal they
passed in time to a higher, attaining complete independence of the heathen, and being ruled by their own
kings.　But they appear to have forgotten the value of
this liberty, in allowing their kings, in default of children,
to adopt the native princes as their heirs.　Thus when
the Portuguese arrived, their Christian sceptre was no
more than a venerable relic, and as such they presented
it to the Portuguese admiral.

The most interesting question which the **Moral and**
existence of this Syrian church in India **spiritual state**
can suggest to us regards its moral condition **of the Church of**
and its testimony to Christian truth amid **Malabar.**
the darkness of heathenism.　It is of little comparative
importance that it numbered an army of 40,000 men, or
that it could show among its relics the sceptre of
Christian kings.　In considering the efforts made in India
by Roman Catholic missionaries, in the name of Christ,
we naturally inquire with special interest, what measure
of Christian knowledge was possessed by natives of the
land which these strangers had invaded ; what standard
of morality prevailed among the Christians of Malabar as
compared with the standard of Rome.　**Comparison**
From the fountain head of Judea, on the **of Western and**
borders of Europe and Asia, the gospel had **Eastern**
flowed out in many streams, to the East **Christianity.**
and to the West.　The streams of the West had,
with the exception of the most eastern, been absorbed in

one swollen, turbid river; those of the East continued to flow in many channels, but their waters, if clearer than that of Rome, were sluggish and shallow. The energy of Europe, of the city whose Cæsars had conquered the world, had made an empire of Christianity, an empire whose subjects were zealous for their own enslavement, and in whom obedience to conscience, or to God alone, would have been treason against the world church and punishable with death. Nothing like this had bound the churches of Asia. Perhaps the force of character necessary to produce it was not to be expected from the Asiatic mind. No doubt something of tyranny, and much of servile obedience might be found among the patriarchs and the people of the Asiatic churches; but, for the most part, there was liberty unknown to the churches of the West. This, however, was not enough to ensure the continuance among them of the spirit of primitive Christianity. The leaven of the East might not be that of the West, but the one was as much a reality as the other. The force of human will in the Papacy might enslave, and almost destroy European Christianity at the very time when it was sickening in Asia, through the sloth and fatalism of the Eastern character. This was, in fact, what had happened in the two churches which were brought into contact with one another by the Portuguese invasion of Malabar. In point of doctrine, the Syrian Christians would have borne comparison, favourably, with any church in the world; but the existence of primitive truth amongst them may be accounted for, at least in part, by that character of quiet sameness which makes the Asiatic of to-day dress like his ancestors of a thousand years ago, while the fashions of changeful Europe have passed through ten thousand varieties. If the truth acknowledged by the Syrians had been held in the spirit of the Lollards, or the Vaûdois, there might have been no need for Protestant missionaries to India; but the history of the church of Malabar brings out no traits of character worthy of the faith which it professed.

We would not, however, deny all credit Good points in to the Syrian Christians for the mainten- the character of ance of Christian doctrine. If there was the Syrians. little spirituality of mind among them, there was at any rate a morality of life which contrasted equally with the manners of the heathen and those of the Portuguese settlers. They were noted for temperance, sobriety, and chastity; for honesty in business and general fidelity. They were courteous to strangers, and deeply imbued with respect for authority; and although constantly armed and trained in the use of their weapons from early childhood, they were the most peaceable of subjects. Moreover, their strength and courage, for which they were held in high estimation by friends and enemies, were beautifully blended with gentleness of disposition, which showed itself in charity to the poor among them and in kindness to their slaves. They were so closely allied to the Armenian Church from the days of their second founder, Thomas Cana, that we might reasonably expect them to resemble the Armenians strongly in character and in doctrine. Their doctrines have been preserved to us by Romish historians and ecclesiastics, and we find in them the resemblance we should have expected; so in spite of the grievous faults which the history of the sixteenth century proves against the bishops and leaders of the Syrian Church, we may hope that the late existence of truth among them was in part the result of that constancy in the national character which distinguished the Armenians for many centuries in enduring Mahometan oppression and resisting the corruptions of Rome.

But few of the traditions of men Doctrines of which had become part of European the Church of Christianity had found their way into the Malabar. creed of Malabar. Originally tainted with the error which had the name though not the sanction of Nestorius, regarding the person of our Lord, they had abjured it in becoming Jacobites, and they were then sometimes.

accused of having gone to the opposite extreme by adop-
ting monophysite views regarding the person of Christ.
They grounded all their opinions upon Scripture,
denying the necessity of any other authority. The pope's
supremacy was usurpation to them, and the peculiar
doctrines of Rome a corruption of the faith. This being
the case, it is not necessary to specify the many points
on which they differed from the Portuguese monks and
priests. The latter held sacred the accumulated mass of
opinions which successive popes had added to, and by
which they had nullified, the gospel; while the Syrians,
in their quiet isolation, having no motive for adding to
the Word of God, preserved the letter of it, at least, in
much of the integrity of Apostolic days. Yet there seem
to have been spots of almost heathen darkness among
the churches of Malabar; as on one occasion the native
prince, himself an idolater, rebuked them sharply for
their neglect of their own religion; and on another, men
professing to be Christians were found divested of every
idea of Christianity, and knowing no worship but that
which they offered to a picture of an old man, a young
man, and a bird. Bad as this was, it will not appear to
enlightened Protestants to be much worse than the
wisdom of the Romish priests who undertook to instruct
them, and explained that the object of their adoration
represented the Father, the Son, and the Holy Ghost.

Having thus briefly sketched the political condition
of India and the character of the Syrian church at the
beginning of the sixteenth century, we now follow the
course of the history which tells us how   History of the
the vanguard of the armies of Europe es-   Portuguese
tablished itself in the land of the Hindus.   settlement on
The natives were for the most part quite   the coast.
ready to give the Portuguese a friendly reception; and so
was their sovereign, the Zamorin of Calicut, the descendant
of Ceram Peroumal in the most important branch of his
family. But the Mahometans, in this opening chapter

of Indo-European history, showed the jealousy and hatred of Europeans which they have so often manifested in later times, and which had so much to do with the great revolt which threatened the extinction of British power in India in 1857. By their influence the Zamorin was persuaded to treat the Portuguese as enemies, and on the arrival of their second expedition under Cabral, the factory which they had built was seized, and all the Europeans who were in it were put to death. The Portuguese admiral retaliated by burning Mahometan ships, and the town of Calicut; and sailing southwards to Cochin, he obtained a friendly reception from the rajah of the district, and concluded a treaty between him and the King of Portugal.

It is not consistent with our subject to enter into all the political details which resulted in the firm establishment of the Portuguese power on the western coast of India. We may observe, however, that it was not effected without the leadership of men of genius and daring. This becomes a striking fact when we notice a similar one in the history of both French and British India. It is not the inferiority of the Eastern races alone which accounts for the immense success of European arms. Sikhs, Affghans, and Rohillas, and even Mahrattas and Mysoreans, have proved themselves formidable enemies to British soldiers on many a well-contested field. Not unfrequently it has happened that the gallantry of the men has barely saved them, while sometimes it has failed to save them from the destruction with which they have been threatened, by the incapacity of their officers, and the imbecility of civil governors has in every presidency been the cause of national shame and loss. But a few great leaders do much. Dupleix and Bussy came near to founding a French Empire in India, which, if it had been established, would have been the result of their political and military genius; and no one who knows the desperate danger from which British statesmen and

The genius of the Portuguese and other Leaders.

c

British generals have, by God's permission, rescued our
cause in the East, can say that the absence of Clive or
Hastings or Wellesley would not have ensured our
sharing the fate of Portugal or of France.   Pacheco and
Almeyda successively maintained the Portuguese foothold against a native army and the fleets of Egypt and
Guzerat; and Albuquerque, who followed them, being
a man of yet larger views, and fit to rule an empire,
seized and fortified the island of Goa, 240 miles south of
Bombay, Malacca in the eastern peninsula, and Ormuz
in the Persian Gulf; and maintaining himself in these
places by means of numerous armed factories and a
strong fleet, raised his country at once to great consideration among all the native princes.   Albuquerque
seems to have been beloved as much as he was feared,
and therefore possessed elements of greatness and claims
to honour which few men of any race in India had
shown in the sixteenth century.   But this did not
prevent him becoming one of the many martyrs whose
memories the histories of France, Portugal, and even
England in the east, have to preserve to their countries'
shame.   The scaffold, the prison, the long-protracted
trial, or the cruel contempt of neglect, have rewarded in
all these countries, some of the most able and devoted
of their Indian servants.   He was happy indeed, if such
an one was then to be found, who served a higher master
than these fickle kings.   Of the European
nations who have established themselves
in India, the French alone seem to have been
animated throughout by the desire for
territorial aggrandisement.   In spite of the
immense extent of British India, and the

*European
nations—excep-
ting France—
had no desire
to found an
Indian Empire.*

many charges made against the statesmen and soldiers
into whose hand it has fallen, it is now an unquestionable
fact of history, that territory has been thrust upon Britain
by an inevitable necessity rather than usurped by her.
There is little merit to be claimed for this, since the one
thought of the directors of the East India Company, who

were no part of the British Government, was to draw as
much wealth as they possibly could, and it was their
general and very reasonable opinion, that the acquisition
of territory, and the wars it would involve, were but
questionable honours, for which they might have to pay
largely out of their own treasury.

The Portuguese seem to have been influenced by
similar motives. They were determined to maintain a
monopoly of Indo-European trade, and so swept the
seas with their fleets from Malacca to Persia and Arabia ;
but they seemed to have preferred armed factories to
tracts of land, and to have made little or no attempt to
increase their settlement at any distance from the coast.
That this was by no means the consequence of any
respect for native rights they showed plainly by their
assault upon the harbour of Diu, belonging to Guzerat, in
1528. Their immense preparations on that occasion
resulted in failure, through the great efficiency of the
native artillery. This fact would seem strange to those
who think of western Europe as always foremost in
modern military inventions ; but the fact that cannon
were first used by the Turks at the siege of Constantinople,
in 1453, and that the Mahometan powers in India were
in easy communication with those of Europe, makes the
superiority of Guzerat intelligible. The invaders were,
however, shortly afterwards successful in establishing an
armed factory in this harbour, partly by treaty, and
partly by force ; and their maritime power, increased by
this means, caused so much jealousy among the
Mahometans, that the Sultan at Constantinople united
with the King of Guzerat and three of the native princes
of the Deccan to expel them from India. Immense
efforts were put forth in this expedition. Great combined
About three hundred thousand men assailed attack upon the
the ports of Diu, Goa, Choul, and Chale, Portuguese.
and it seemed an impossibility that the few regiments of
Europeans who garrisoned these places, and who, in the
case of Diu, were reduced before the end of the siege to

forty fighting men, could maintain their ground. But the desperate valour and military genius of the soldiers of Europe, saved them, in all cases, from what appeared to be inevitable destruction. From that time the Portuguese were almost unmolested by the Indian powers. Men who could fight such battles, and stand such sieges, were not lightly to be quarrelled with. And so the energy and warlike spirit which had been exercised in fighting Mahometan fleets, and Hindu armies, needed a new direction and a new object.

Missionary enterprise offered to supply the necessity. It was no new thing for the spirit of conquest and chivalry to be offered on the altar; for men whose lives were "earthly, sensual, devilish," and whose hands were continually imbrued in blood, to become the self-elected champions of God. Bad as men are, nothing stirs their minds more generally than religion. Ignorantly, presumptuously, they decide for themselves what is truth, or accept what is offered for it by the traditions with which they are most familiar. But whatever they really believe becomes a power on the life, so that those who have a creed in their hearts are ruled and driven by it according to the strength of their passions, or the susceptibility of their minds. Pure religion—the heaven-born gospel of Christ alone—changes the man before it uses him. All other religions, being powerless to do this, must use him as he is. They may, and do develop much that is there already, pouring oil upon the flame of his zeal, and quickening the energies of his soul. But these energies are merely natural, and are often the slumbering enemies of God and men. If religion finds a man brave, she makes him absolutely fearless; if he is obstinate, she makes him as one deaf and blind; if he is cruel, she fits him to be an inquisitor. Hence we do not wonder that the followers of Mahomet should be earnest to make converts, and that they should do so with the sword.

[marginal note: The energy of Portugal directed to Missionary enterprise.]

[marginal note: General influence of Religion.]

The fierce tribes of Arabia, united by a religion of enthusiasm, could not be other than fierce enthusiasts. But it is strange to see men contending in the same spirit, if not with the same weapons, for Him who came to manifest that "God is love," and who charged those who would be His disciples, if a man smote them on the one cheek to turn to him the other also. Yet this sight has been a common one in the Christian Church, even from the earliest ages, and the page of history we are now to glance at records one of a thousand examples of it. We have always to bear in mind that professors of Christianity are not necessarily Christians, nor is Christianity chargeable any more than "Liberty, Equality, and Fraternity" with what has been done in their respective names. We have seen that she was little known in Europe, in the fifteenth century, and so we do not expect to find her reigning in the colony of Portugal. In opposition to the method of Mahometanism and false Christianity, the true action of the gospel is expressed in one brief and divine sentence, "Speaking the truth in love." Here there is zeal for God and man, and no energy is too great to be consecrated to this service. It allows, yea, charges a man to be "instant in season, out of season, reproving, rebuking, exhorting," but it must be "with all long-suffering and doctrine." To such a spirit, coming in contact with Hinduism, or even with the church of Malabar, all true-hearted men would wish God speed; but such was not the spirit of Portuguese settlers and Romish missionaries.

Yet at the very outset, and having stated the rule, we must notice a notorious exception. Francis Xavier was the first Romish missionary of note in India. For forty years before he commenced his labours, priests and monks had been plentiful in the Portuguese settlements. But for the most part their zeal had found other expression than preaching to the natives. Xavier, although a Romanist—a Jesuit—an apostle in the eyes

Xavier an exception to the rule just noticed.

of his church, cannot fairly be taken as an example of
that church. He stands alone in the picture of his times,
a strange, but noble figure, suggesting sad thoughts of
misdirected energy and superstitious zeal, yet refreshing
the mind that has been studying his contemporaries with
traits of love, and pity, and self-denial which one may
look for elsewhere in vain. Ignatius Loyola had just
founded the "Society of Jesus," and Xavier was one of
his first and most illustrious converts. But we cannot
introduce our sketch of Xavier's labours by an account
of Jesuitism. To do so would be to flatter an evil
system, and to disparage a great man. The ignorance,
the superstition, the false doctrines of Rome, are no
doubt, abundantly illustrated in the life of her Indian
apostle, but with all these there was in Xavier an
uprightness of character, a denial of self, a devotion to
God, and a sympathising tenderness which forbid us to
characterise him morally as a Jesuit. We shall therefore reserve our notice of the Society which came to the
aid of tottering Rome, and which gave Xavier to India,
until we have to consider the missionary efforts of men
who were Jesuits indeed.

Yet Xavier was the champion of Rome, **A view of**
who went forth to do battle with idolatry, **the Religious**
and therefore we cannot well go beyond **systems of**
this point in the history without glancing **Europe**
at the religious aspects of Europe and of **and India.**
India, and endeavouring, as briefly as possible, to
manifest the essential character of the two systems of
Hinduism, and Romanised Christianity. Neither of
these systems was built in a day. As to the latter, it
had been growing for nearly a thousand years when the
sixteenth century began. Bad at the best, and corrupted
during all those ages by elements of evil which never
ceased to work destruction, it had at that time, by all
testimony, arrived at a climax of apostacy and wickedness. The supremacy which had been sought by
ambition, and obtained from a murderous emperor ;

which had been confirmed by the false Decretals, and
used for the extinction of national and individual liberty,
had enabled the mistress of Christendom to pervert the
gospel as she pleased, and to add doctrine after doctrine
as she found them conducive to her interests. In this
way Roman Christianity became more and more corrupt
till "the whole head was sick, and the whole heart faint,
and from the sole of the foot, even to the head, there was
no soundness in it, but wounds and bruises, and
putrifying sores." At the dawn of the sixteenth century
its representative was Pope Alexander VI, a man whom
the cardinals of that day were not ashamed to set up as
the vicar of Jesus Christ, but whose existence would not
now be tolerated in the most depraved and lawless
society of Western America.

There was no crime of which this supreme bishop was
not guilty. And if history can supply an example of a
more monstrous criminal, it is his illegitimate son, whom
he trained in vice and made an archbishop and a
cardinal. Europe had long been prostrate at the feet of
Rome ; now Rome herself lay bleeding at the feet of the
Borgias. The "holy city" was the nest of robbers and
assassins ; no man's life was safe whose wealth could
tempt the insatiable avarice of the Pope or his son. Yet
the Church, which had chosen this leader, allowed him to
reign in peace ; nay, in many of its members, enjoyed
and approved his rule, because he paid his servants
punctually, and patronised the arts ; and he died at
length unmolested, through accidentally drinking of the
poison he had prepared for a company of his courtiers
whose wealth he meant to possess. This was the Pope
who sent Christianity to India, the kings of Spain and
Portugal having sought and obtained from him a bull
authorising them to hold exclusively their newly-
discovered dominions, "*with a view of propagating the
Christian religion among the savages by the ministry of
the Gospel.*"

We could almost suppose the Papacy had been in the
hands of deadly enemies during the election of this
Pope; for surely the bitterest hatred, and the keenest
satire might have been well expressed in such an
appointment. But in truth there was nothing more
needed to produce the amazing exhibition, than that
Popery should be left to itself. " God gave them up,"
as He did the heathen world before, " to a reprobate
mind." Lies in doctrine produced sin in life, and sin
grew by its own nature and because that which produced
it grew until it became too big to be concealed, and then
there was nothing left but to sin without shame, to call
darkness light and light darkness.

It might be unjust to form our opinion of the religious
condition of Europe entirely from the character of the
Pope and the state of Rome, although no one can
reasonably doubt that these were indications of a corrupt
state of the church, and that they must have immensely
influenced the morals of the people. But unfortunately
we have overwhelming evidence that Alexander VI and
his cardinals were true representative men of their age.
The state of Rome was no accident, but the result of the
system which reigned with equal sway in Italy, Britain,
and Portugal. Everywhere the regular clergy were
avaricious, depraved, and tyrannical. The monks, who
were no better, and if possible, more ignorant, ate up the
lands like swarms of locusts; and from these the
common people learned their religion by means of the
blasphemous mummeries of miracle plays and the
lives of their teachers. The only antidote to the evil, the
Word of God, was an unknown book; so that the will
worship and the traditions of men prospered without
hindrance. Here and there a few might groan in secret
over the state of the church. A man of learning and
heart religion like Grostête, might dare to protest openly
against the laxity of morals; and the poets Boccaccio,
Dante, and Petrarch, might picture the purgatory of
wicked popes. But these protests were no more than

the stones in the bed of the torrent, of which the smaller
are borne along, or lie unnoticed at the bottom, while the
greatest can do nothing to stop its course. Such was the
religion of Europe, when Europe undertook the conversion of India. Nothing could be more unchristian
than such Christianity.

We have only further to inquire whether there were
any circumstances in favour of Portugal which might
make it appear that she was at all better fitted than
other Roman Catholic nations of the age to Christianize
a heathen country. There were none. She was as fit
as any to be an example of the religion we have described.
Moreover, we have testimony to the character of the men
she sent out to India—testimony not of later Protestant
writers, or of enemies, but of Roman Catholics of their
own age and country. And besides this, the unquestioned
facts of history which we must pass in review needed
for their accomplishment the hearts, and minds, and
hands of the zealots of Popery.

The description given by Roman Catholic
writers of life in Portuguese India is
sufficiently horrible, and yet it is acknowledged to be but a part of the truth.
The state
of Society in
Portuguese
India.
Profligacy reigned without fear or shame, and shared her
authority with violence, treachery, and atheism. One of
the severest censors of his own countrymen was the
Carmelite missionary, Vincent Marie de S. Catherina,
distinguished for his efforts to put the yoke of Rome on
the neck of the Syrians ; yet this very man applauds
the people whom he persecuted with as much earnestness
of language as he uses in denouncing the wickedness of
the members of his own communion. It is true we
must not charge the Church of Rome with all the immoralities of her people ; and it may be said that the
state of English society in India 150 years ago was no
compliment to Protestantism. But there is this difference
between Romish and Protestant colonies, that the former
have the means of religion, such as they are, established

among them, while the latter very frequently have not.
The British settlements in India were long without so
much as military chaplains, not to speak of missionaries
or other ministers. Their spiritual interests were shame-
fully neglected, and the result was a general immorality.
But this may surely be more reasonably charged upon
the absence than upon the presence of Protestantism.
It was very different with the colonies of Portugal. They
were never without priests and monks professing to be
armed with Divine authority and power to communicate
the influences and blessings of the church. Therefore,
according to the doctrines of Rome herself, they would
be responsible for the moral and spiritual condition of
their people to an extent which could never be the case
with Protestant churches.

Let us now consider those Indian nations Religious
which Alexander VI. desired to convert to condition of
mediæval Christianity. The " savages," India.
as he called them, will bear comparison with their
missionaries. This, however, is not saying much, nor is
it possible to say much in favour of Hindu or Mahometan
morality. Turning from Europe to India, we look from
one dark picture to another. It is difficult to say which
is the worse unless we consider the comparative opportunities and responsibilities of the two, in which case
we must certainly condemn Christendom. But neither
had that superiority which would have justified it in
undertaking to teach the other, yet we find that each
assumed this in turn ; the Mahometans, who afterwards
reigned over India, teaching Islamism to Europe at the
point of the sword, and the warlike children of the
West returning the assault in a similar spirit, in these
missions which we are now considering. The mass
of the people of India, however, were quite free from
such thoughts of religious conquest. Brahminism was
the gift of the gods to them alone, and no stranger could
be joined to them in any one of those castes into which

the gods had divided them. But what was
Brahminism? And what moral character
did it produce in its adherents? The first
of these is a difficult question to answer briefly. One
might travel throughout the length and breadth of India,
examine its splendid temples, observe the worship of the
people, and listen a thousand times to the poems in
which they celebrate the doings of their gods, without
understanding the fundamental idea, the original
philosophy of Hinduism. By such experience one
would necessarily learn much of the moral character of
the people, enough to distress and to sicken those
who had lived in the healthy atmosphere of true
Christianity; but one would probably be baffled in
the attempt to discover the scheme of man's wisdom
which had resulted in such a manifestation of sin and
folly. For this knowledge we must go to the ancient
writings, which are to India what the
Bible is to Christendom. Even this, however, does not make the task an easy one.
If, instead of the Scriptures, our authority were the
entire works of all the Fathers of the first five centuries,
we should hardly depend upon such a ponderous mass
of theology as that contained in the "Great Shastras" of
the Hindus. It has been said that "the longest life
would not be sufficient for a single perusal of them." It
would be irrelevant to our subject even briefly to describe
their contents. We may, however, convey some idea of
their size by noticing that the Puranas alone, which,
together with the great epic poems of India—the
Ramayan and the Mahabharat—constitute one of the
eighteen subdivisions of the sacred books, contain about
two millions of lines, while the poems we have mentioned
run on through half a million more. The whole of these
Shastras are declared to be of divine authority, some of
them having proceeded directly from the mouth of the
creating deity, and the rest being a revelation from him,
through the medium of other gods or inspired sages.

The very language in which they are written is sacred, and, in the hands of the most divine race of the Brahmins, carefully guarded, like a precious locked casket with the treasure contained in it, from the presumptuous handling of other men. It has thus been ever difficult for a Brahmin, impossible for any other Hindu, to examine for himself the religion of his own Scriptures. British authority, and the labours of great European orientalists, have, however, now brought to light enough to show clearly the true system of Hinduism, and to bring to the bar of public opinion the philosophy which is chargeable with the moral degradation of India.

There are men in India now, men of note and influence, the religious leaders of young Bengal, who contend earnestly that the first religion of their country was a pure deism, a soul-satisfying worship of the one true God ; and who, preaching a theology which has been suggested to them by a one-sided view of Christianity, declare it to be the faith of the venerable Vedas. This is utterly untrue, and the authors of it, if honest men, must be strangely deceived. They teach what they desire to believe, but what has been proved by incontestable evidence to be without foundation. The Brahminical religion of India never was anything else than Pantheism. It may not have been—nay it was not—in the earliest days, the elaborate system which now makes room for three hundred and thirty-three millions of divinities, but it was that which naturally produced all that now exists, which made the idolatry and the ever-increasing polytheism of modern times a possibility and a necessity.

Pantheism the original Philosophy of the Vedas.

It is true the first conception of this venerable religion was that of one supreme God, and that the sacred writings often speak of this being in a manner that might lead us to believe his worshippers could acknowledge no other. He is described as eternal, immutable, immaterial,

The Nature and Attributes of the Supreme Brahm.

invisible ; almighty, omniscient, and omnipresent, and as
enjoying unspeakable happiness. But there is nothing
in all these words, or in the many others which the
sacred writings apply to Brahm, to satisfy the common
desires of men with regard to the object of their worship.
There is nothing to call forth devotion, or fear, or hope,
nothing to accept or reward their services ; for the Indian
Brahm is absolutely without moral qualities, and, in his
present and proper state, without so much as the
consciousness of his own existence. His happiness is
that of a profound and dreamless sleep. Hence there is
no such thing in India as worship of the one supreme
God, nor was it ever intended that there should be.
The philosophy which imagined Brahm was under the
immediate necessity of imagining other gods as objects
of worship, and to fill the place in men's minds which
could never be filled by a confessedly unconscious
divinity. But although new gods are brought upon the
scene by Hinduism, the Hindu shastras continually
assert that Brahm alone exists. Apart from him there is
not, nor ever can be, any animate or inanimate being.
This is very plainly teaching that all which does exist is
God, and it is just this which Hinduism intends to teach.
Brahm, say the Vedas, after ages of repose, awakes out
of sleep, and wills the existence, or rather manifestation,
of the universe. Properly speaking there is no creation
in this. The god says, "Let me be many ; " and all that
springs into apparently new existence at his will is but
an endlessly varied manifestation of himself. In this
way the triad of Hindu gods, first drawn forth from the
supreme, Brahma, Vishna, and Shiva, is a triple
reproduction of Brahm for the further development,
preservation, and destruction of the universe. To the
same source the three consorts of these gods owe their
separate existence ; the sensuous ideas of Indian
philosophers supposing such sexual variety a necessity
for the comfort of the heavens, and the government of
the earth. While all the schools of Hinduism agree as

to the character of Brahm, and the eternal priority of
his existence, and while the idea of creation out of
nothing has never entered the mind of any Hindu, there
is great variety and, indeed, hopeless confusion of theories
as to the actual history of the manifestation of the
universe. We need not introduce here even the outline
of more theories than one ; it is enough for our purpose
to know the basis of the popular system of worship.
We may, however, notice, in order to make more plain
the essential Pantheism of India, that all orthodox
Hindus reject the doctrine of the eternity of matter as
opposed to spirit, as well as that which represents matter
and spirit as blended together in the nature of one God.
Moreover, that a common belief among orthodox Hindus
is, that as spirit cannot create or even influence matter,
that which we call matter has no real existence whatever,
but is an illusory appearance of a purely spiritual reality.
According to the popular mythology which   Sketch of the
is grafted on one or other of the philo-   popular
sophical systems professing to be taught   mythology.
by the Vedas, the entire universe was developed from
"the mundane egg," which the supreme god, in one of
his hours of consciousness, produced by assuming in
turn a male and female nature. Before the formation
of this egg, however, all the principal elements necessary
to the fully developed universe had been educed from
Brahm directly or indirectly ; the difficulty so troubling
to the Hindu mind regarding the action of spirit upon
matter being supposed to be overcome by the doctrine of
the grosser elements being evolved from those less gross,
which again owed their origin to more spiritual essences,
the most purely spiritual of all being the intellectual
principle which flowed directly from the Divine source
itself. The egg being formed, and all these earlier
productions being collected within it, the supreme being
entered it in the form of Brahma, and occupied 430,000,000
years in bringing it to maturity. At the end of that
time he burst forth in divine splendour and visible form,

accompanied by the complete universe with its many worlds. These worlds were next peopled with their respective inhabitants—celestial, earthly, and infernal. The energy of Brahma is described as exercised in this work. He strives and fails, then fasts and mortifies himself in order to success. He rages and weeps over repeated failure, and nearly faints away at the sight of the monstrous creatures which find existence in his tears. At length he succeeds both in heaven and on earth. He makes more gods to rule India than men and women to regard them. Evil is personified more than good, for it is easier to imagine the former than the latter. Gods of lust and theft and folly and cruelty, as well as some of a better character, call for the worship of men. Every action of life, however ordinary, however trifling, is put under the supervision of one of these. Everything is religion, yet nothing is spiritual, scarcely anything moral. The future rewards of obedience are of three kinds, the lowest being an upward step in the transmigration of the soul, which, however, may at any time fall back again by subsequent failure. The second is a temporary and sensuous enjoyment of one of the higher heavens, after which the soul returns to its labours. And that reckoned the highest of all—to be attained only by an extraordinary course of self-mortification and abstraction of the mind from all earthly things—is the absorption of the soul in Brahm, —is, in one word, annihilation. For the punishment of the wicked there are 100,000 hells, in one or another of which the offenders against Hinduism are tormented, according to their guilt, for a few years or for millions. But annihilation is the final end of all. What the saint may attain at the close of life by his virtues is the consummation of all virtues and vices, all rewards and punishments. After millions of ages, and many periodical deluges, Brahm is again as at the beginning. The entire universe is gone, returned to its original source. Brahma, Vishnu, and Shiva are blotted out as

truly as their votaries and as the material worlds, and
nothing remains—though Hindus declare that exactly
the same amount of existence remains—but the supreme
god sunk in his dreamless sleep.

It is not difficult to see what the **Necessary effect**
character of a nation must become under **of Hindu**
the influence of such a religion as full- **mythology.**
blown Hinduism—a religion which insists on being felt
every hour by its slaves of every caste; which keeps
ever before them the lustful lives of its demon gods in
the endless poems which celebrate their deeds, in the
shameless representations of the same upon the walls of
their temples, and in the association of one or other of
them with every circumstance and every state of life.
A people will never rise morally above its gods, provided
it really believes in them. And if Hindus were to con-
form themselves to the example of their best and most
favourite divinities—Vishnu in the incarnation of
Krishna—they would think very lightly of theft and
indecency. The ordinary temple worship is, as we
should expect, marked by a moral filthiness which can
never be fully described to a people of Christian
sensibilities. Troops of " sacred " prostitutes are an
essential feature of this worship, while one of the
commonest objects of adoration throughout the whole of
India, by men and women alike, is the indescribable
" Lingam," of Thiva. It is inconceivable that a nation
should remain for ages under such influences as these
without sinking below the average state of human
depravity.

Moreover, apart from the examples of **Effect of the**
their gods, and the immoralities connected **original**
with their worship, the original philosophy **philosophy.**
of Hinduism was of itself sufficient to deaden the conscience and to paralyse the mind in any struggle with
evil. In its consistent Pantheism it denies that man is
a servant to God, and teaches him to consider his
relationship that of a part to the whole. As Brahm must

be everything, predestination accounts for all that is bad,
as well as all that is good in the world, so that man has
no free will, and therefore we might reasonably add,
little conscience, no merit, and no guilt. And if nature
so far survived these theories as to persuade the Hindu
that his future in some measure depended upon himself,
he found little to encourage him in the meagre reward
held out to a lifetime of tedious ceremonies, or in the
assurance of a common final annihilation to good and
bad, to gods and men.

Such was the religion of India when it was invaded
by Roman Catholic Christianity. Such had been its
influence upon its millions of people, when the men of
Portugal and of Rome landed upon their shores. The
absurdities of Hinduism have, no doubt,
often caused a smile; but if we would   Lessons which
learn something from them, we must see,   may be learnt
not a subject for mirth, but an awful and   from Hinduism.
humbling proof of the vanity of man's philosophy in the
matter of religion. The men who laid the foundation of
the system we have been considering were no thought-
less savages, or wild dreamers, or collectors of distorted
traditions, but men of mental power and earnest
meditation,—men who were dissatisfied with the con-
clusions of the philosophers who preceded them, and
who dared to grapple anew with the great problems
which none had hitherto been able to solve. They were
men who would know the nature of God, the origin
of evil, the history of matter, and who dwelt upon
these questions until they thought they had found an
answer; and their scheme was as reasonable in its
first conception as those of other rationalists who
have ventured self-confidently upon the same ground.
They could not, any more than these, satisfy the
heart or allay the fears of guilty men, and hence
others quickly built upon their foundation a monument
to their shame.

D

We need hardly say that no systems **Comparison of** could present a greater contrast than true **Hinduism and** Christianity and the Pantheistic idolatry **Roman** of India. Yet we cannot but see many **Christianity.** points of resemblance between the latter and the Christianity of Rome. In direct contrast with the Gospel, which proclaims salvation by grace through faith alone, Hinduism and Roman Catholicism exalt man's works, the one as the only means, the other as the principal means of obtaining the favour of God. They are two great systems of self-righteousness; but when we come to examine the righteousness which they produce, we find there is nothing more in the one case, little more in the other,—except when light from without raises the soul above the system of Rome—than a round of trifling ceremonies, without any moral or spiritual element. Both Hinduism and Romanism, in their fuller and later forms, were made by the priests to magnify themselves at the expense of the people. Their persons were sacred, their interests considered in all things, their enrichment identified with service to God. In order to secure the people's dependence upon them both in Europe and in India, they kept the sacred books in a language which the people did not understand, and thus they were able, without shame and without opposition, to prescribe and to demand what they chose, although in the one case it was directly opposed to the teaching of the Bible, and in the other found no place in the most sacred of the Shastras. We shall have occasion to notice hereafter how some Romish missionaries practically acknowledged the resemblance of the systems in their adoption of heathen rites. But, apart from this, the church of Rome had for ages been teaching Brahminism to Europe, and the Brahmins Romanism to India, in the pilgrimages, and ablutions, and penances, and self-mortifications with which both systems endeavoured to satisfy the most sensitive souls, and to quiet the most uneasy consciences.

No religion is so dangerous as that which most closely imitates the truth. Romanism must necessarily imitate the truth in order to have a standing at all, because its origin is primitive Christianity. Imitation of truth in Hinduism and Romanism. Hinduism has no such connection with revelation, yet we find truth strangely copied from time to time, even in the midst of its bold Pantheism and monstrous idolatry. God, it teaches, is all and everywhere; His worship and service are the true life of man; nothing is too little to offer Him, nothing too great. There is enough of the image of truth here to carry home even to many inquiring minds the lie upon which it is painted. But what a contrast have we in the result of its reception to that produced by the Christian teaching from which it might seem to have been borrowed — "to live is Christ" — "whatsoever ye do in word or deed, do all in the name of the Lord Jesus, giving thanks unto God and the Father by Him."

Before leaving the subject of the moral relationship which subsists between Hinduism and Romanized Christianity, we may notice one point in which they are the complements one of the other, and in which together they afford, perhaps, the Each of the two systems the complement of the other in relation to a spiritual truth. weightiest of all examples of a great truth of Holy Scripture. That truth is, that the natural man cannot find out God, nor even retain the knowledge of Him that has been given by revelation. He "understandeth not the things of the Spirit of God, neither can he know them because they are spiritually discerned." And, again, as "the carnal mind is enmity against God," it "does not like to retain God," that is, the true God, "in its knowledge." Hence Hindu philosophers struggled in vain to account in a reasonable way for God and His works, and "professing themselves to be wise, they became fools." Hence, too, worldly and merely nominal

Christians who succeeded the apostles and earliest bishops of the church, in spite of the mid-day splendour of Gospel light, fell gradually back into midnight darkness.

There being so little to choose between Hinduism and true Romanism, the efforts of the Pope's missionaries and prelates cannot much engage the hearts of the lovers of truth. And yet none of these, we think, have been able to read the story of Xavier's life without some feelings of love and admiration, or without a measure of shame that such zeal as his has so often been wanting in the bearers of the Gospel of salvation. While it is certain that a belief in the doctrines of Rome tends to destroy all faith in God, and so to prevent **Bright exceptions in the Church of Rome to the spirit of Romanism.** the fruits of the Spirit, history affords us many examples even in the darkest ages of men, who neither knew nor sought an escape from the apostate church, taught by the still small voice in their hearts. Thus Grostête could sit as bishop of Lincoln, and denounce with indignation, made weighty by a holy life, the corruptions of the papacy. Thus Curione, and Vergerio, and others of the "Renaissance" could walk for a time in the land and within the Church of Rome by a light which Rome could never have given them. We believe Xavier's heart was moulded by the hand which moulded theirs; nor will any one who marks the wonders of God's ways, or who remembers that He is able to fill one "with the Spirit from his mother's womb," find it inconceivable that the Romish saint and apostle should also have been a humble child of God, and a believer on Jesus. He had not the light which enabled Fra Bernardin Ochino to preach, in his cowl, salvation to the crowds of Venice. His soul was never electrified by the concentrated truth of God's message to the monk of Wittemberg. But if, on this account, his usefulness was not to be compared with that of Gospel preachers in the Church of Rome,

the Christian elements of his character shine out, in the
gloom which surrounds him, with the greater brilliancy.

Yet we are far from considering Xavier,   *Danger of*
apart from his work, as a satisfactory   *exaggerating*
Christian. If his heart was tender with   *the virtues of*
the love of Christ, his mind was darkened   *Xavier.*
·by belief in Rome; and that belief, held with all
his eager enthusiasm, produced grievous incon-
sistencies of character. Moreover, the story of his
life has no doubt been grossly exaggerated. If we
receive it from the biographies of Roman Catholic
writers, we must believe in apostolic miracles, in super-
human exertions and sufferings, and in unprecedented
missionary success. If, on the other hand, we would
learn it from his own letters, and turn to those annual
epistles which he wrote to his friends in Europe, we are
likely to be deceived by a burning earnestness and by
sentiments of piety which are greatly qualified by the
thoughts of the same writer in his more frequent and
familiar intercourse with a missionary friend. In these
last letters we see the man; a character more real, if less
divine, than other authorities would make him, and yet
so great as to justify the admiration we have expressed.

Xavier was born in 1506, in one of the   *Birth and early*
noblest families of Spain. His home was   *life of Xavier.*
an ancient castle in the kingdom of Navarre,
where he spent a somewhat lonely and contemplative
youth. At seventeen he left his father's castle for the
University of Paris, where he studied philosophy with
native talent and characteristic earnestness. The result
was agreeable to his ambition. He became a Professor
and Lecturer, and his lectures won him some fame. He
was at that time as unlikely as any man to adopt an
exclusively religious life. But there was one watching
him whose eye had detected the enthusiasm and nobility
of his character, and who possessed one of those master
minds which control the wills of other men, and change
the direction of their lives. Ignatius Loyola was at

Paris, lodged in the College with Xavier. Ignatius Loyola.
One of the most chivalrous of soldiers, —his influence
cast out of his profession by honourable on the life of
wounds, he had devoted his life to spiritual Xavier.
warfare. The Knight of Spain, the gay courtier
and gentleman, had passed off the scene, and the
Knight of the Virgin occupied his place, in the guise
of an eccentric mendicant. That mendicant, shrunk
from with horror, or hooted at in derision, was laying the
foundations of a kingdom which was to exist in the
midst of all kingdoms, and to trouble them all. Probably
at that time he was unconscious of the greatness of the
system his hand had begun to form; but he knew the
materials that were most valuable for any great and
enduring building, and he set himself patiently to collect
them. He did not work in vain at Paris. He went to
it one man, and left it ten—ten men of one mind and
heart, individually great and fitted for great things, but
ruled absolutely by the will of the original Ignatius
Loyola. Xavier was not easily won. The world smiled
upon him, and Ignatius called for separation from the
world. Faber, the former swineherd of Savoy, surrendered
quickly; but the proud and high-born Spaniard in the
midst of his philosophy, disliked and ridiculed the
ignorant enthusiast. Yet Ignatius, in his ignorance,
was stronger than Xavier with his philosophy, and, in
spite of the resistance of the latter, the walls were
undermined and the fortress taken. Patient endurance
and acts of timely kindness compelled the young
professor first to admire and then to love; and in the
intimacy of hearty friendship, the fire of Loyola's religion
kindled an equal flame in the heart of Xavier. Whether
the grace of God was at this time communicated to the
future missionary or not we cannot say, but there is
something very like the working of the Holy Spirit in
this incident of these men's lives. Ignatius, with his
deep human wisdom, had been expressing joy at his
friend's success; then, as if musing in himself had added,

" But what is a man profited if he gain the whole world
and lose his own soul ? " That word, whatever was its
really spiritual power, was mighty for Ignatius and for
Rome. It converted the professor of philosophy into the
apostle of the Church.

Protestant influences are said to have   **"Heretical"**
been at work on Xavier before the arrival   **influences on**
of Ignatius. The reformation had its   **Xavier.**
converts and supporters in Paris, and with some of these
he may have become familiar ; but the language in which
he refers to his heretical acquaintances would be more
applicable to the freethinkers of the School of Lorenzo
de Medici, which the revival of letters had created, than
to the sober and godly followers of Luther and Calvin.
He says of Ignatius, when introducing him to his elder
brother in Spain, " The benefit he has conferred of
highest value is that of fortifying my youthful imprudence
against the deplorable dangers arising from my familiarity
with men breathing out heresy, such as are many of my
contemporaries in Paris in these times, who would
insidiously undermine faith and morality beneath the
specious mask of liberality and superior intelligence."
It is quite possible, however, that Xavier, under the
influence of Loyola, might speak in these terms of men
whose Protestant faith and morality ought to have
commended themselves to his conscience, and at the
same time that he might have learned from them some
lessons of truth which his heart and life retained after
he had cast off as heretics the men who had taught
them.

Three years more Xavier spent in Paris,   **Ignatius and**
and three with his confederates in Italy—   **his associates**
the latter period as a poor friar, tending   **in Italy.**
the sick in the hospitals, and preaching a revival of religion
in the universities. Then came the call to his great life-
work. The king of Portugal heard of the   **The call to mis-**
new order which Loyola had founded, and   **sionary work.**
the piety and zeal of its members. He

was dissatisfied with the monks of the old type who had
been sent out to India to win souls, and had done little
but care for their own bodies, so he begged the entire
society from the Pope, and the Pope was ready to give
it. But Loyola had a will of his own, which neither
Papal supremacy nor Jesuit vows could set aside; and
as he did not want to go to India, or to part with the
weapons with which he meant to conquer the world, the
king and the Pope had to change their minds. Loyola
gave them two of his party, and a fever seizing upon one
of these, more generously substituted Xavier, with whom
his general would not lightly have parted. With the
devotedness which ever characterized him from the time
when he renounced the world at Paris, Xavier yielded
joyfully to what he believed was the will of God. But
through the long and many delays of those times, it was
more than two years before he set foot in India. There
was room for missionary work, however, on the way.
Ten months at Lisbon, and six at Mosambique, offered
many opportunities of doing Christian service, and
Xavier used them to the utmost of his ability. In May,
1542, he landed at Goa, where he is said (with no
improbability) to have spent the whole of the first night
in devoting himself to God, and praying for blessing on
his labours.

And now, what were those labours, and The labours
what the amount of blessing which of Xavier
accompanied them? We have seen that in India.
we cannot rely on the accounts of the Romish biographers of Xavier, and that we must trust for infor-
mation almost exclusively to his own letters; moreover,
that the rose-coloured tint of his yearly epistles, written
in the exciting atmosphere of communion with Loyola
and the great ones of Europe, is apt to deceive us, and
therefore that, while we may count on the truth and
honesty of the writer, we must look for the picture of
his heart and life to more homely correspondence.
Facts Xavier will always give faithfully, and to those

facts we now turn. For five months after his arrival in India he remained at Goa, discharging the functions of a priest of Rome, but adding to these a constant and earnest testimony against the vices of the nominal Christians of the place, and a strenuous endeavour that appears to have had some measure of success, to lead them into something of Christian morality. But great as were his zeal and purity of life, they were not accompanied by that stability and triumph of faith which have distinguished so many Protestant missionaries in years of discouraging labour. We find him continually moving from place to place, and when we seek in his letters an explanation of these movements, we meet with so many expressions of disappointment and impatience, such open avowal of failure, that we are obliged to believe he was more led by vague hopes of better success in further and yet further fields, than by the principles of apostolic evangelists. Before he arrived at Goa, a college had been founded for the education of natives in the doctrines of Rome, with a view to their becoming the Pope's missionaries to their countrymen. The college was not finished, and there were neither students nor applicants for admission ; but the want was already supplied by Rome's easy way of making Christians and missionaries : a number of children had been procured, who were, by the divine will and transforming power of the church, to be fitted to convert the thousands of the heathen. Xavier gave much attention to this college and obtained the transfer of it to the Jesuit Society. Before half a year had passed he was in another field of labour. This was the pearl fisheries of the Paravars, in the **Mission to the Paravars.** neighbourhood of Cape Comorin. The choice of this region was not of Xavier, but of the Portuguese governor, Don Alphonso de Soza, who had a scheme in his mind, to create a united nation of these scattered fishermen, who had already, under Mahometan oppression, purchased the protection of the Portuguese

by a promise to become Christians. Even before
Xavier's time, 20,000 of them had, according to the
Jesuit authority Tursellinus, been baptised by Romish
priests, who immediately after left them to themselves.
For a year Xavier laboured among the Paravars, having
the encouragement of performing thousands of baptisms.
He knew nothing of their language, nor did he ever
acquire it; for, nearly two years after this time, during
a later visit to this same people, he describes in one of
his letters his helplessness in the midst of a population
of an unknown tongue, without the assistance of an
interpreter. He adds that he ought to be an adept in
dumb show; but that nevertheless he is not without
work, since no interpreter is needed to baptise infants
just born, or those which their parents bring, or to
relieve the famished or the naked who come in the way.
The absence of his interpreter on this occasion was
owing to sickness. Xavier freely availed himself of such
help whenever he was able; and indeed, according to
the Jesuit Bouhours—the loudest of his panegyrists—
he had much need of it; for, says that authority, "in
truth he spoke very badly, and his language was but a
confused jargon of Italian, French, and Spanish." With
the picture of Xavier's helplessness before them, drawn by
his own hand, it needed the boldness of Romish casuists
to declare, as in the process of his canonization, that
"when he visited people of various tongues, which he
had never learnt, he was in the habit of speaking their
language with as much elegance and fluency as if he
had been born and educated in the countries, and it
often happened that when men of different languages
composed his audience, each heard him speak in his own
tongue."

One of the most familiar passages of his **Description of Xavier's mode of preaching.**
letters describes the way in which he
laboured on his first visit to the Paravars.
He was accompanied by several boys from the College at
Goa, and was joined in the midst of his work by a

coadjutor from Europe named Francis Mansilla. His first care was to have the creed, the Lord's prayer, the ten commandments, and the Ave Maria translated into the language of the people ; his next to commit them to memory. He then commenced his visitation of the different villages. Twice a day, by the sound of a bell, he called the inhabitants together, repeated to them what he had learnt himself, and exhorted them by his interpreters to listen so as to remember it, and, when they had done so, to go home and teach the words to their families and to their neighbours. The people soon learnt to follow him in his repetition, and readily professed a belief in every article of the creed as he separately pronounced it. By such means, together with baptism, "he made many Christians," but he found reason afterwards to doubt whether they so much as understood what they had professed to believe, as they had been commencing their repetition of his words in the creed with "volo" instead of "credo." However, they were gladly reckoned Christians by the Romish Church, and there is no reason to think they were inferior to the generality of her converts among the heathen. But Xavier had too much Christianity in his own heart to allow him to be satisfied with such converts. However he had got the measure of truth he possessed, he did not know how to communicate it, and so it is no wonder that, although he ever retained a pitying love for these poor Romanised Paravars, he soon turned to seek for better success, not only in other districts, but among Hindus of a very different class.

His next effort was directed towards the Kings and princes of India, in the hope of their influence and example being the means of nations being born in a day. But here again he was doomed to disappointment. For several months he remained at one spot, seeking to obtain an interview with a sovereign whom he called "the great king of

His attempt to influence the native princes.

Travancore," and who was probably no other than the
Rajah of Bisnaghur, whose extensive dominions we have
already noticed.   But neither Kings nor Brahmins
would own the sway of the apostle of Rome.   However,
Xavier gained something by these negociations for his
poor friends on the south-east coast. They had suffered
grievously since he left them, from the incursions of a
people spoken of as the Badages, who were probably the
army of the great king which collected his royal dues
from the fifty-six turbulent kingdoms which owed him
allegiance.   They had vowed the destruction of the
Paravar Christians, and attempted it with too much
success.   Xavier flew to their relief, a work   **Xavier**
most congenial to his generous nature, and **succours the**
by his timely help, and wise arrangements, **poor Paravars.**
together with such influence as the "King of Travancore"
could exercise over his lawless soldiery, they were
restored to some measure of comfort and safety.   Failing
with the great, Xavier had no alternative while he
remained in India but to continue his labours among the
poor ; and he did this in his usual spirit of zeal, tenderness, and superstition, in different parts of southern
India, between Goa, and the district of the Paravar
fishermen.   In Travancore especially he made a great
number of converts, and it is of his visits to that
kingdom that one passage in his letters asserts that he
baptised 10,000 heathen within the space **Questionable**
of one month.   The fact, however, that this **statistics of**
statement occurs in only one of his **baptisms.**
letters, while four others were written at the same date,
of which one was to Ignatius Loyola, and another to
the King of Portugal, makes it very doubtful whether
Xavier was the writer of the passage in question.   The
extravagant and shameless manner in which his
panegyrists have invented experiences and miracles to
do him honour makes it far from improbable that some
other hand than his inserted these high-sounding

statistics. Moreover, the "very many Christians" of whom Xavier does speak as the fruit of this visit he acknowledges to have been the converts of a native Christian, who accompanied him, rather than his own, for he recommends this man to his friend, Mansilla, as one who "knew perfectly the manners of the people, and the means and precautions which it was necessary to take with them," and charges him to do as he himself had done in following his advice, and letting him do whatever he judged to be expedient.

But the Apostle of Rome, notwith-   Xavier's standing these successes, was longing to disappointment leave India. He was disappointed in the in India. natives, both kings and fishermen, and disgusted with his own countrymen, whom he called "the filth of the human race." He expressed to Mansilla an intense desire to turn his back upon the land where he had expected to live and die, and to sail away to Ethiopia; but one hope detained him a little while. The native Christians of Manaar, a small island near to Ceylon, had been cruelly persecuted by their heathen king, and hundreds of them had been put to death. Xavier, who had always one hand for politics, and a heart for sympathy, threw himself eagerly into the matter, not to console the sufferers by the Word of God, and such aid as he had obtained for the Paravars, but to punish the rajah of Jaffnapatam by the fleet and army of the viceroy. His heart burned with indignation and hope, for he considered this a time for the destruction of the wicked, and for the building up of a Christian kingdom. The expedition was rapidly planned, and Xavier hastened again to the south, to be ready to enter the door which the sword of Portugal would open. But what was done in worldly wisdom for the cause of Christ was frustrated by the worldly wisdom of others. The seizure by the offending king of a Portuguese vessel with a rich cargo put an end to the expedition; for the governor preferred peace, and the recovery of his goods, to a doubtful war with an.

apostolic benediction. Xavier now hastened
away from India. It had no further
attractions for him, and he persuaded himself that it no longer required his services.
His letter written from Amboyna, in the
eastern seas, says he had taken care that the Comorin
Christians should have no lack of spiritual aid, and that
those of Ceylon, not far from Cape Comorin, were
" admirably instructed by two Franciscans, and as many
priests." "Other native Christians," he adds, "who are
in the Portuguese cities, are instructed by the means of
the bishops.   As soon as I perceived that my labours were
not at all needed in India, I went to St. Thomé on my
way to Macassar." It is very striking that in this apology
for leaving India, Xavier makes no mention at all of the
work of evangelising the heathen, and this silence agrees
well with a passage which occurs in one of his letters
written at a later period—"Believe me, trust my experience,
all our ministry to this nation reduces itself to two
capital points—the baptism of children, and their
instruction as soon as they are capable of it."

He leaves India, and satisfies himself that he is no longer wanted.

His labours elsewhere than in India do
not come within the limits of our subject.
For nearly two years and a half he
travelled throughout the Chinese Archi-
pelago, doing little more, according to his own account,
than "searching through all the localities of the Christians" who had been made by earlier missionaries,
confirming these in what they already believed,
"baptising very many infants," and establishing the
influence of the Jesuits wherever it was possible.   He
returned to Goa in 1548, again disappointed; for the
inducement to make this long voyage had been the
reports which he had heard of the readiness of the
islanders to receive Christianity, and of the conversion
and baptism of two heathen kings.   The character in
which he chiefly appears during the period of his
second stay in India, which extended to fifteen months,

His voyage among the Eastern Islands.

is that of a general superintendent of His work as
missions, and a commissioner of the king Head of Romish
of Portugal. We gather from his letters Missions in the
that he exercised over all Jesuits in India East.
an authority as unlimited as that of Loyola over the
whole Society. He planted and supplanted men as he
pleased, and enjoined upon them constantly the Jesuit
duty of implicit obedience. At the same time his authority
was always exercised with such courtesy and tenderness
as to prevent all suspicion of pride and self-seeking.
Besides the missionaries of other Roman Catholic orders,
there were now more than twenty Jesuits who had
entered upon the Indian field of labour. These were
not all settled on the mainland of India, but were
distributed by Xavier among the principal stations held
by the Portuguese in the eastern seas. By his authority
at this time the Jesuits acquired for their Indian mission
that pre-eminence which they held with characteristic
skill and tenacity until Rome herself became ashamed
of their enormities. The influence which he possessed
in secular matters, through the friendship of the king of
Portugal, Xavier used as freely as his ecclesiastical
powers. He gave directions regarding the trade of the
pearl fisheries, and recommended to royal favour persons
of various classes, from the poor priest to the governor,
whom he thought worthy of promotion, and threatened
with punishment, which he was fully able to execute,
those who were of a different character.

Very soon after his return from his Interest in
long voyage among the islands, Japan Japan. The
became the great object of attention to Japanese con-
Xavier, and he embarked for that country vert Anger.
in the summer of 1549. No event in his missionary
life is invested with such true interest as this; none
has so much appearance of the Divine approval and
arrangement. Here we have, to all appearance, a true
convert to Christ brought out of heathenism by means
of Romish missionaries or traders, and then leading and

accompanying one of the former to his native land, that
they might together pour the few rays of light which
they possessed upon its darkness. This convert was a
Japanese gentleman named Anger, who had killed a man
in Japan, and had left his home as much from distress
of conscience as from fear of discovery and punishment.
A Portuguese merchant, from whom he sought help and
counsel, advised him to go with him to Malacca, where
Xavier was supposed to be labouring. The Japanese
readily assented, and according to his own account,
received so much Christian instruction from the merchant
by the way, that he was ready, had circumstances allowed,
to be baptised on his arrival at Malacca. He was disappointed, however, in his expectation of finding Xavier,
and therefore attempted to return to his own country.
But after being within sight of land, a violent storm
drove him back to the port from which he had sailed in
China, and there he was found by two Portuguese, one
of whom was his earliest friend, and was advised by
them to turn again towards Malacca. This time Xavier
was found, and the Japanese was at once joined to him
in a lasting friendship. They proceeded to Goa, where
Anger received such further Christian instruction as the
Church of Rome could give, including at least the
gospel of Matthew, which he learnt by heart, and where
he, and his servant who accompanied him, were afterwards baptised. The letter in which this Japanese
convert gave an account of himself to the Jesuit Society
at Rome is very interesting, and presents a contrast in
its Scriptural simplicity to many of the epistles of his
teachers, especially to the manual of instruction which
Xavier must have written about the same time for the
native converts he was again about to leave. The latter
is characterised by the grossest superstition, and some of
the most absurd of the fables of Rome, while the letter
of the Japanese, which is of considerable length, contains
not one word, excepting the names of persons and places
connected with the Romish Church, which might not

have been written by an intelligent Protestant convert. One passage will show satisfactorily that this one heathen at least may be reckoned to have been led into the fold of Christ, whatever was his connection with an apostate church—"Now that God, the Creator of all things, and Jesus Christ who died on the cross for our salvation, have thus furthered our undertaking, we trust that all may turn out to His glory and for the propagation of the catholic faith. I am every day more and more convinced of the truth of the Christian religion, both by the many mercies which God has lately granted me, and by the deep peace which I experience through my whole soul." With this companion,—honest and zealous like himself—and four others, Xavier entered upon his mission to Japan.

Again our subject forbids us to to follow him into the details of his success and failure, but we may notice that he had **Xavier's visit to Japan.** more than usual experience of the former, the first harvest being from among the relatives and acquaintances of Anger; and that often, as far as we can judge, by no other means than by communicating doctrine, and sometimes by the help of diplomacy and presents to a native king from the Portuguese viceroy, considerable numbers were led to a profession of Christianity and the rite of baptism. These were greatly increased in numbers by missionaries who followed in Xavier's footsteps, so that when persecution broke out on account of the new faith, the Christians were strong enough to maintain the struggle for forty years, and when, after that time, in 1637, the emperor, like the catholic king of France, ordered a general massacre of his dissenting subjects, 37,000 of them are said to have fallen at once. But of all this great numerical success, a very small share must be attributed to Xavier. He was never able to speak the language without an interpreter, and when, at a later period, he was preparing to enter China, where he might reasonably have expected a similar result, he

E

said, " I shall succeed in opening it for others, since I myself effect nothing."

Xavier was two years and three months in Japan, and he returned to India in January, 1552, after an absence of nearly three years. It was his last sojourn in India—a short and a painful one. In less than three months he was on his way to China, more glad than ever, no doubt, to escape from a land where he had been so bitterly disappointed both in the heathen and in his own countrymen, and where, on this last occasion, he had experienced the heaviest grief of all, in the scandalous behaviour of the only men in whom his confidence had hitherto remained unshaken, his fellow-associates of the society of Jesus. He desired to make his voyage to China a political embassy, and for this purpose, making free use of his influence with the king of Portugal, he took with him a merchant in the character of an ambassador. The reason for this arrangement was that all foreigners were forbidden to enter China on pain of death. But the governor of Malacca, the successor and brother to one who had always befriended Xavier, spoilt his plan, seizing upon the ship and forbidding the enterprise. Xavier had no alternative but to abandon the mission or to go alone. With true courage, though with questionable wisdom, he chose the latter course; but neither the crown of martyrdom, nor the honour of a successful ministry awaited him in China. He died on the Island of Sancian, within sight of the land he was not permitted to reach.

His return to India, and last sojourn there.

Death of Xavier.

The circumstances of Xavier's end remind us of the death of Henry Martyn. Alone in the midst of the heathen, in wretched cabins, where soul and body sympathised in the absence of every comfort, and on the threshold of the land they had toiled in love to reach, each of these men of missionary fame breathed

Some comparison between Xavier and Martyn.

out his spirit into the bosom of God. And the death scenes are not the only ones in which we see a resemblance between Martyn and Xavier. It is true there must ever be contrast between a missionary who in his testimony knows "no man save Jesus only," and one who preaches, together with Jesus, as many intercessors as the idols of the heathen. Yet, as we have seen, there is abundant reason to believe that Xavier's heart was true to God, and that the faults of his character and of his ministry arose from no want of devotedness, but from the influence of the apostate Church, which failed to pervert more completely the servant of whom she was unworthy. Xavier was educated at Paris, Martyn at Cambridge; the fetters of the former were rivetted by the fascination of Loyola, the liberty of the latter was consecrated by the ministry of Simeon. That Xavier, in Henry Martyn's circumstances, would have been a less noble example than he of missionary service and self-sacrifice we cannot say. From the time when he first gave himself to the work, believing that he was called to it by God, there was no going back, no abatement of his self-denying zeal till he breathed his last within sight of China. Disappointment there was, and in consequence frequent changes of effort and of purpose; and the charge of inconstancy has thus, with some reason, been preferred against him. But we would rather see such apparent inconstancy, which showed the dissatisfaction of his heart with the work which was all Rome could enable him to do, than that courage and perseverance which distinguished later missionaries of his order, who settled for thirty or forty years in one spot, absorbed and contented with the labour of turning Hindus from the idolatries of India to the idolatries of Rome.

In considering the character of Xavier as it appears from his labours, we have only seen the evil which resulted from the superstitions of his church, and the good

Further consideration of the character of Xavier.

which the man possessed in contrast with that church.
One or two points, however, remain to be noticed before
we can form a right estimate of the greatest of Romish
missionaries. During the whole of his life in India he
was protected by the power of the State, and armed
with its worldly weapons. He was the commissioner of
the king of Portugal, the legate of the Pope, the
representative of Ignatius, and the intimate friend of
all. And these powers were no mere honours paid to
the zealous champion of the Church. They were
intended to be used over the bodies and souls of men to
coerce them to the truth, and for this purpose Xavier
gladly accepted and constantly used them. It may be
true that when he sailed from Portugal, the guest of the
Viceroy, he declined all the comforts that were liberally
provided for him, and fared more meanly than the
meanest on board. This was quite in accordance with
the character of the man. But what Xavier would not
use for himself, he would use with all freedom and
earnestness for the cause of the Church, and, as he
would think, for the cause of Christ. And so we find
him reproving, rebuking, exhorting, not with all long-
suffering and doctrine, but with stern threats of punishment by the arm of the State. Thus the Portuguese
Governor of Tuticorin, whom Xavier regarded, no doubt
with reason, as a hinderer of Christianity, was threatened
by him with "the utmost rigours of the Inquisition";
and the Head-men of professing Christian villages were
exhorted to morality of life under pain of being carried
in chains to Cochin, and suffering perpetual banishment.
But we would qualify the censure which some have
passed upon these proceedings of Xavier, by suggesting
that there is, or should be, such a thing as discipline—
which implies punishment—in the Church, and that the
confusion of secular and ecclesiastical powers, and the
reckoning of all worthless professors, and of whole
nations, as Christians, created a difficulty in the ad-
ministration of discipline, which could not have been

solved by anything less than the condemnation of the
hoary system which was the recognised Christianity of
the world.

Moreover, liberty of conscience was a thing unknown
and unprofessed in Christendom in Xavier's century.
If men dissented from Rome, and millions did so, they
did not dissent from her principles of uniformity and
coercion, but from her corruptions in life and doctrine,
and her extravagances of cruelty. And when they had
power themselves they used it, in milder forms of
persecution, against all who differed from them. Thus
William Prince of Orange and founder of the Dutch
Republic was charged with culpable laxity, and even
suspected of atheism, because he judged, in opposition
to his Protestant countrymen, that every one should be
free to worship God according to his own conscience.
It is sad indeed to have to associate the name of Xavier
with the hellish tribunal of the Inquisition, but it is a
happy and interesting circumstance that his tenderness
and generosity of character shine out conspicuously in
his intercourse with the very man whom he had
threatened with its horrors. The Governor of Tuticorin
shared the fate of the poor pearl fishers of Cape Comorin,
being reduced to the greatest extremities by an invasion
of the Badages. Xavier no sooner hears of his distress
than he writes with the greatest urgency to his fellow-
worker, Mansilla, to "fly to his relief." There is as
much anxiety and sympathy and wise considerateness
in this letter, the subject of which is his bitter enemy
and the enemy of religion, as there is when he is
describing the sufferings under similar circumstances of
those who were his children in the faith. After giving
minute directions regarding the assistance to be rendered
immediately to the Governor, Xavier adds, " I would go
myself if I could believe that my arrival would be
agreeable to the Governor ; but he lately renounced my
friendship, writing letters full of atrocious complaints, in
which, among other things, he asserted that he could not

even mention without scandal the wickedness which had been reported to him concerning me. God and men know whether I ever did him any evil, especially such as he cannot speak of without scandal; but this is not the time for vindicating myself or complaining of his conduct. As to our present business, it is sufficient to know that he has such feelings towards me that I ought, for his own sake, to avoid meeting him, lest I should add to the grief of a man in his misfortune, and, by the sight of one whom he hates, increase a calamity already sufficiently great." Such a letter as this is alone sufficient to establish the nobility of Xavier's character. Those who understand the greatness and the rareness of Christian charity, will know how to estimate it. Had the Pope and the cardinals, who seventy years afterwards put Xavier's name in the calendar of saints, remembered how much better such a characteristic was than speaking with the tongues of men and of angels, they might have found a respectable excuse for canonising their missionary without shamelessly fastening upon him a reputation for miraculous gifts which contradicts all the testimony of his letters regarding himself.

To conclude our remarks on Francis Xavier, we may notice in a few words what he did in India. He baptised very *Summary of his work in India.* many converts to Rome, but for the most part they were those who before his arrival had bargained to adopt the Portuguese religion on condition of receiving Portuguese protection. Sometimes he had influence among the heathen, as in one case where he baptised a whole village in consequence of the impression made by the recovery of a woman who seemed to be dying in her confinement, and for whom he prayed; but no second instance like this, as far as we know, occurred in India. He rebuked and exhorted his own countrymen with much faithfulness, especially the great among them, and set before them the example of a pure and self-denying life. He opened the way for the Jesuits in the East, and obtaiued for them pre-eminence among all the missionaries of Rome. For this last part of his work he would not now obtain either credit or thanks from Roman Catholics or Protestants. His influence over his own countrymen, in checking their immorality, there is reason to fear was but slight and transitory; and his converts among the heathen were such as to cause him to despair of India and of all missionary labour, and to propose to his sovereign to make the conversion of the idolators the business of the officers of the State. While, therefore, there is much that claims our admiration and sympathy in the character and life of Xavier, there is little that remains in the searching hand of truth to justify the boastful praise which Rome has lavished on her greatest apostle.

Let us now turn again for a few moments to Europe. For as the missions abroad were always in communication with the church at home, and as the life and strength of the former were constantly *A view of Europe and the Papacy, after the pontificate of Alexander VI.* supplied by the men and briefs received from the popes, the successive phases and the history of the Papacy in Europe cannot be irrelevant to an account of its labours among the heathen. The true character of Roman Catholicism comes out more clearly under the high pressure of European politics than when a number of individuals are seeking with worldly wisdom to recommend its system to nations of other religions. Moreover the followers of Ignatius Loyola, of whom Xavier is too good an example, begin now so to crowd upon the scene of Indian missions that we want to know something more about their character as a Society, and the events which made them necessary to the Roman Catholic Church. They were one of the greatest phenomena of the sixteenth century, and the salvation of the Papacy.

The last view we had of Europe was in the pontificate of Alexander VI., whose bull was the authority of the

earliest Portuguese missionaries. We would now rapidly
trace the history of Rome from that date to the time at
which we have arrived in India, where those veteran
troops who had saved the popes are already beginning
to show that the followers of Loyola are not followers of
Xavier, and who, with the greatest profession of obedience,
will presently assume as bold an independence as Luther,
and carry their only authority within themselves in the
will of their superior. Julius II. had succeeded " the
infamous Borgia ; " ferocity personified following the
representative of lust. Leo X. was the next great
shepherd of the Roman Church, a man of pleasure, and
something very like an atheist ; a patron of philosophers,
but still more of buffoons ; distinguished for the blending
in his court of paganism and catholicism, and for the
sale to the credulous world without of the right to
commit the sins which the heads of the church indulged
in without expense. This was the pope who was opposed
to Luther, not a likely antagonist to conquer Divine
truth and German obstinancy. There was hope for the
papacy under Adrian VI—hope of prolonged existence,
for cure was impossible, as that honest pope seemed to
know, when he complained that the disease was in the
head, and spread thence throughout the whole body.
But Rome would not be saved, if salvation meant nauseous
medicines and moderation in sins ; and so Adrian died
having effected nothing save gaining the hatred of his
church and the respect of his enemies. Yet though
Rome was glad to bury Adrian, there were those in the
church who saw that the alternative was reformation or
destruction, and who set themselves in the next pontificate
to try to cleanse the Augean stables. But their efforts
were in vain, and the next pontiff, Clement VII., was
not the man to help them. The Capuchins strove to
exorcise the demon of heresy by self-inflicted mortifications and midnight vigils, but it continued to defy
them. The Theatines, more practical, and in many points
strongly resembling the Jesuits who followed them, went

into the battle under the generalship of Gaetana da Thiene and Caraffa, and did good service in a spirit of courage and asceticism. But Rome was not cleansed, and the voice of the Theatines was lost in the din of other arms than those of Luther. Clement would fight like an earthly prince, and like an earthly prince he fell. The soldiers of Germany crossed the Alps, sacked Rome, and besieged the pope in the Castle of St. Angelo. The moral effect of this fall was felt throughout Europe. Clement, who could turn with the wind, made peace with his conqueror, and hoped to retrieve his fortunes ; but craft deceived him, and he fell more heavily than before, this time with the loss of England. These political difficulties, with the graver ones of religion, he bequeathed, after twelve years' reign, to his successor, Paul III., a less moral man, by repute, than himself, and a slave to astrology. Paul was forced by his helplessness to call a general council, and, in his desperate circumstances, determined in some sense to reform himself and his court. A commission to investigate abuses, with Caraffa as a leading spirit, painted the papal portrait with no flattering hand, and the horrible diseases of the church. The church listened to its report, but winced and recoiled, and decided that the time had not come for such strong measures as Caraffa proposed, and pleaded the extent of the disease as a reason for more gentle treatment. Thus this last effort failed, all the resources of Rome having been tried in vain on her behalf except one, which she knew not, and of which the spirit only was yet in existence. The unknown reserve was Ignatius and his Jesuits.

The fortunes of Rome had never been at so low an ebb since she had assumed the triple crown as they were when Ignatius stepped forward as her champion. The revival of learning as the earthly means, *Low state of the Papacy which made the opportunity for Ignatius Loyola.* and God Himself as the spiritual power, had waked up millions from the bosom of the ignorant and sensual church. The Reformation spread throughout Europe,

everything that was good and true, if only secular,
striking a blow for it against the tottering Papacy.
Rome had no arms to withstand these assaults. She
thundered, but her lightnings were harmless to most of
her enemies. She had reigned as the queen of darkness,
but darkness was flying before the light. Knowledge
had penetrated not into Germany and England only, but
into Italy itself, and some popes and cardinals had
played with the novelty, strangely ignorant or forgetful
that knowledge meant heresy, and heresy meant
revolt. Had Rome possessed knowledge to meet
the knowledge of the Reformers, and an appearance of
morality to rival their morality, the battle might have
been equal; but such weapons were not to be found in
her armoury, nor did it seem likely that any one could
furnish her with them. But the Jesuits brought her
these and more, and by the genius of Ignatius Loyola
communicated life and energy to the palsied and
moribund Papacy. We have already seen Ignatius at
Paris, gathering to himself the choicest fruits of its
university. With these he presented himself to Paul III.,
and was accepted; not, however, as the founder of a new
order, or as General of the Jesuits; for Ignatius, though
he had made his plans three years before, was too wise
to startle the Pope and to make enemies by proposing a
new order of monkhood at the very time when half
Europe was in arms against those already in existence.
He offered himself and his friends to the service of the
Pope, to preach in public, and teach children, taking no
pay, but living on alms, lodging in hospitals and seeking
God only. Three years' trial satisfied the Pope, so that
in September, 1540, he established the   Rise and
order of the Jesuits, and in 1543 he progress of the
removed the restrictions with which he   Jesuits.
had qualified the first charter. The growth of the
Society from the beginning was prodigiously rapid.
When it was three years old it contained eighty members,
the greatest number which was contemplated by the first

bull of Paul III being sixty. Three years more sufficed
to create ten Jesuit establishments in various parts of
the world, and another period of the same length
increased the number to twenty-two. The Society was
not seven years old before it was the chief power in
Catholic Christendom, the object of curiosity and
admiration to all ranks of society, courted by kings and
learned men, and manifestly indispensable to the Pope.
The Jesuits earned their fame: they were no mere
favourites chosen by caprice. They offered to do a great
work, and they did more than they said. They stirred
Europe and the world for the Papacy; stirred it, not as
St. Dominic or Peter the Hermit had done, but as it never
had been stirred before or could have been by any but
the children of Ignatius. Their weapons were not papal
bulls and flaming faggots, although they had a place for
· these; nor were they the words of enthusiasm, although
enthusiasm was not wanting. They fought by intellect,
and learning, and craft which even the sixteenth century
with its new found strength—century of Luther and
Erasmus, of letters and of Protestantism—was unable to
conquer. The Council of Trent gave Ignatius an early
opportunity of showing the world the value of his Jesuits.
Two of the Society attended as the special defenders of
the interests of the Pope. Protestant truth appears in
some measure to have illumined the Augustinian
monks, the old associates of Luther, for their General
attempted to demonstrate to the Council something like
the Reformer's doctrine on the subject of Justification.
But the learning and eloquence of the Jesuit champion,
Laynez—the former of which appears in the account we
have of it absolutely super-human—overwhelmed all
opposition, and re-established the old Christ-dishonouring
doctrines of Rome. Laynez fell ill with his labours, and
the Council, astonished, admiring, and grateful—while
the world waited impatiently for its decisions—suspended
its business until the Jesuit's recovery.

Equal prodigies were being performed on other fields

by this devoted band. They were everywhere in Europe, and in Africa, America, and India besides. Their schools grew into colleges, their colleges into universities. At Coimbra alone, in 1551, they were moulding 150 students. The year following, the Rector of Salamanca university preferred a place in their novitiate to one in the college of cardinals, and high-born and learned men—among them Francis Borgia, Duke of Gandia—had long preceded him. In the midst of all the stir, the fame, and the labour, side by side with the Roman pontiff stood Ignatius Loyola, the man of boundless ambition yet imperturbable calm, governing as never pope or emperor the forces which he had created; directing and controlling, by his gigantic mind and will, the energies of all his Jesuits in every corner of the earth. The forces of Loyola were those which above all others strove to establish Roman Catholicism among the heathen. Rome has had no missionaries in the East who for earnestness, perseverance, and abilities, can stand a comparison with the Jesuits. It is therefore important to our subject briefly to enquire what a Jesuit is, as distinguished from   A Jesuit as a other missionaries and other men. He is   man and as a a picked man to begin with. Great as are   missionary. the influences that are brought to bear upon him when he submits himself to Jesuit training, he must have evident talent, to be developed and directed by that training. Wealth, nobility, good manners and appearance—everything that tells in the world—is valued and sought for, but it will scarcely be accepted without talent, and certainly not without malleability. The unequalled personal influence of Ignatius in the first place, and the hold which his followers quickly obtained, by their training establishments, over the minds of the young, made his choice of good materials easy. But it was not his choice of men, but his training of those who were chosen that displayed most clearly the genius of Ignatius, and that accounts for the strength of his .

society. Ignatius was an euthusiast, at least in the
beginning of his course; but he was far more of a
schemer. He nearly killed himself at Manreza in his
desperate efforts to surpass the fakirs of the desert in
their frightful asceticism; but when he had recovered
from these mortifications and the season of delirium
that followed, he had the ability to collect the experiences
of both, and to weave from them a sytem of mental
education which he called "spiritual exercises," and
which, if it put the most learned Frenchman of the day
mad, broke the wills and governed the spirits of
thousands, and attached them, with a power which no
other human system has possessed, to one another and to
their general.

It would be out of place to discuss here   **Chief**
the "spiritual exercises" of Ignatius, or   **characteristics**
the "Constitutions" of his Society, which   **of the**
   "Spiritual
were the other great means of bringing   **Exercises"**
into the world that almost indescribable   **and the**
class of beings so well known and feared **"Constitutions."**
under the name of "Jesuits." But we may notice that
the chief characteristic of the former, which consisted
in a course of meditations on the principal subjects of
Christian doctrine as taught by the Church of Rome,
was its power of impressing the senses with things which
are wholly spiritual, and so of appearing to triumph over
nature, and to lead men into perfection, when in truth
their hearts were altogether unchanged; while the effect
of the latter was to produce and to strengthen continually a desperate selfishness, which defied or explained
away every law human or divine that barred its progress,
but of which the self was not the individual man, but
the Society in which he was taught to forget his individuality.

Thus, in the new phase of Catholicism   **Power**
there was much outward morality, and   **necessarily**
what the world mistook for holiness, while   **possessed by**
  the new Order.
the volcano of human depravity was

burning within ; and there was much labour and
patience and suffering in the name of God and of the
supposed head of his Church, with the one real motive
of glorifying the order of the Jesuits.   No wonder, then,
that 20,000 of these men, carefully chosen and skilfully
educated, bound together by common training and
common separation in heart from all but the new self of
their Society, should do great things, and should even
govern the world for a time.   No wonder, either, that
such a system of self-deception should break down in
some notable instances, and, as in the mission field of
China and India, and in every country in Europe, the
men who were the right arm of the Papacy and the idols
of their Church should become objects of universal
execration for utter apostacy and intolerable crimes.

This brief sketch may call to mind the general
character of the Society, which in the middle of the
sixteenth century supplied and directed the energies of
the Romish Church, and whose bands of missionaries
were by that time treading quickly in the path of
Xavier, and passing to the front and to every post of
command and responsibility in India, China, Japan, and
all the colonies of the East.   Yet they were not all bad
men ; the memory of Xavier forbids us   Exceptions to
to think so : and there were others who   the general
were honest as he was, especially those   bad character
who joined him in his Japanese ex-   of the Society.
pedition, and Gaspar Barzans, the Belgian, whose
preaching during a short residence at Goa is said to have
produced a powerful impression on the Portuguese.   We
may reasonably hope that there was a spark of spiritual
life in these men, and that they were the means, notwithstanding their delusions, of kindling such a spark in
the minds of some heathen.   But no doubt they were
rare exceptions.   The story of Jesuitism in India and
China, if we must allow it a place at all, is one of the
very darkest pages in the history of Christianity.

A leading peculiarity of the Jesuit con-   Failure of
stitutions was the absolute and blind   the system in
obedience which they required all members   India.
of the Society to yield to their superiors, and this,
together with the regular and frequent "manifestations
of conscience" which they demanded, and the secrets of
which were all transmitted to the General for practical
use, promised a perpetual cohesion in the Society, and
an absence of all rebellion. But this promise was
quickly broken, at least in India. Rebellion in Europe,
under the eye of Loyola, was, perhaps, impossible. His
influence seemed irresistible, and his anger, when once
roused, was terrible. But India was far from Italy;
and although Loyola had his eye upon the distant mission
field, and knew well how to deal with instances of dis-
obedience, it was long before such could be reported to
him, and before his lash could reach the offender. When
Xavier left India for Japan, he transferred the greater
part of his authority to a Jesuit named Paul Camerti,
who was rector of the college at Goa. But he reserved
for another Jesuit, Antonio Gomez, "full and absolute
power over the novices of the seminary, with the entire
management of the revenue and property of the College."
Xavier had too good an opinion of his fellow-Jesuits.
In communicating his arrangement to Camerti, he wrote,
"From my intimate acquaintance with all the labourers
of the Society of Jesus, who serve God and the church
in these regions, I am of opinion that they do not need
any ruler to guide them in the ways of God; nevertheless,
in order that they may not lose the opportunity of gaining
additional merit by obedience, and since strict discipline
requires it, I think it expedient that they should have
some one to whom they may pay obedience." Vows
are easily broken, even by those who have been subdued
by the "spiritual exercises;" and the "constitutions"
themselves, with their substitution of expediency for
principle, and justification of everything which a Jesuit
could think for the good of the Society, or "the greater

glory of God," taught every member of the Society the
way to break them. Moreover, this division of power in
India was a serious error, and a very
singular one for an associate of Ignatius   **Xavier's**
Loyola to have committed, as it was plainly   **mistake.**
contrary to the main idea of his strong military government. The result was disastrous to the Society. During
Xavier's long absence the two rulers quarrelled, and the
more self-willed, Antonio Gomez, transformed the
missionary college at Goa into a training establishment
of Jesuits, and afterwards removing to Cochin, he expelled
the Franciscans from their college in that place, with a
view of appropriating it to the same purpose. Xavier's
return, however, stopped his proceedings, and the
refractory Jesuit was banished from India, and perished
at sea on the way to his place of imprisonment.

After chastising several other offenders,   **He rectifies it**
Xavier showed that he had profited by   **on leaving the**
experience, and before leaving for China,   **country for**
he did what Ignatius himself would have   **China.**
done, and appointed Gaspar Barzœus, who had hitherto
been stationed at Ormuz in the Persian Gulf, to the
undivided command of all the Jesuits east of the Cape
of Good Hope. Barzœus very soon died, and Xavier
did not survive him. What arrangements and what
labours followed, history very scantily informs us, and
it is not worth our while dwelling longer on the
monotonous details. The character and the work of the
first Jesuits in their efforts among the heathen are
indicated with sufficient plainness by the facts which we
have noticed. It is interesting, however, to know that
even the "Apostle of India" was not uncensured in his
labours. The stern spirit of Ignatius was   **Recall of**
dissatisfied with his reasons for leaving   **Xavier by**
India, and at the time of his death he was   **Ignatius.**
under a peremptory order to return to Europe with all
possible speed, and in the mean time to send home one
of his associates to undergo the examination of the

General. Xavier never received this order. He went
to render his account to God, instead of doing so to the
man who had usurped His place.

While Xavier was baptising his thou- Commencement
sands of heathen, and growing up to the of the attack
stature of a missionary saint and hero, Syrian Church.
other hands were working not less diligently
than his to crown the Pope and to glorify Rome in another
field of labour. It was not to be expected that Roman
Catholics from Europe—Roman Catholics of the sixteenth century—should be content to dwell side by side
with independent Christians who knew nothing of the
Pope, of transubstantiation, or purgatory. To look for
such a thing would have been as unreasonable as to
expect that, in the present age of the world, "the wolf
should dwell with the lamb, and the leopard should lie
down with the. kid." For forty years, indeed, the
Portuguese appear to have left the Syrian Church
unmolested, but this could only have been because their
hands were fully occupied in establishing and maintaining themselves in the country, or because the
Christians at Malabar, with their 40,000 fighting men,
were too large a prey to be openly and hastily attacked.
But a truce is not peace ; and so, as soon as Rome was
strong enough, she set herself to the necessary business
of annexing the Syrian Church. Don First effort
Juan d'Albuquerque—the bishop of Goa by means of
who received Xavier in India, and the the Franciscans.
first who held that office—commenced the operations
of the Romish Church against the Syrians. He was a
Franciscan, and the Franciscans had much to do with
the missions of the century, and would have had more
but that the Jesuits came in everywhere and supplanted
them. Don Juan sent a monk of his own order named
Francis, in 1545, to visit the southern and more
respectable branch of the Malabar Christians, and to
induce them, if possible, to acknowledge the supremacy
of the Pope. The friar took up his abode at Cranganore,

F

and was encouraged by the courtesy and friendliness of
the Syrians, who opened their churches to him and gave
him full liberty to preach. But no converts attested
the power of his preaching, although Roman Catholic
authorities speak highly of his persuasive eloquence ;
and the old historian Geddes shrewdly inquires how it
happened that this father, of whom we hear little
afterwards, possessed in his *first year* in India so much
greater power than Xavier, since he laid no claim to a
miraculous gift of tongues. The Syrians, finding the
Franciscan was an enemy, continued to go their own
way and civilly left him to his ; and as he had even
erected churches in their city, to teach them the right
style for such sacred buildings, they were probably cast
empty upon his hands. But all the servants of Rome
know how to wait when they cannot strike ; and so the
friar, by permission from Goa, founded a college, and set
himself to the task of making Romish priests out of
Syrian youths. Education is always a tempting bait,
and as the Franciscan, no doubt, taught freely, it is not
to be wondered at that some poor Malabar Christians
were found as unwise as thousands of English Protestants
at the present day, and although they would no longer
listen to the friar's preaching, were willing to accept his
lessons for their sons. Whatever else he taught them,
Father Francis took care they should learn the language
and ritual of Rome, and when this was accomplished
they were ordained priests and intended to convert their
countrymen. The Syrians, however, were not prepared
for such sudden conversion. They gave up their
Romanised sons rather than their liberty, and the
Franciscan found the fruits of his college a company of
apostate Syrians who could in no way further his work.
After this experience Father Francis appears to have
despaired of success, and to have abandoned the field to
more subtle and persevering labourers.

The Jesuits read the lessons of his failure,   Attempt of
took up his tools, and went to work in their   the Jesuits.

own way. The college was a good thought, the Latin dress and language bad; and so the men who knew better than any others how to trim to the times, set up a new college about three miles out of Cranganore, and let it be known that they would teach without invading the time-honoured language of the Syrians or altering the dress of their students. By this means another hopeful opportunity was gained. Students came in and submitted to Jesuit influence for the sake of Jesuit learning. But when the fathers sought the results of their labours they were very small. Indeed, they were more dishonourably defeated than their predecessor; for while the Franciscan was foiled by the elders of the Christian community, the Jesuits were outwitted by the lads themselves, who took what they could get, and then prayed for the patriarch of Babylon, and maintained the opinions of their ancient church in the very faces of their Romish teachers. This would perhaps have staggered other men, but Jesuits are not like other men. As Napoleon said of our countrymen on the field of battle, "They don't know when they are beaten"; and so they were not long in trying stronger measures for success. The Syrian bishop appeared to be the great hindrance to the work of proselytism. He possessed vast influence over the Christians of Malabar, governing them in all civil as well as ecclesiastical matters, and therefore having more the dignity of a pope in his diocese than that of a simple bishop. This made it necessary that he should sooner or later be taken out of the way, to make room for the Roman pontiff. It seemed probable, too, that if he were removed at once, some of his people would submit in his absence to their self-elected teachers. The Jesuits had no excuse for laying hands on an innocent man, and the venerable head of an independent church; but such a difficulty has ever been a small one to Rome, and to her Jesuits in particular. With them, might is right; and there was might enough in the Portuguese viceroy, and in the Jesuit influence which governed him, to cause the Syrian bishop to be seized at Cochin, and carried away to Portugal. But, for the third time, the emissaries of Rome were outwitted by the simpler Syrians. Mar Joseph, whom they probably supposed to

Seizure and transportation of the Syrian bishop— Joseph.

be lodged in a dungeon of the Inquisition, or at least to be separated by many thousand miles from his flock, soon and suddenly reappeared in Malabar, a greater man ecclesiastically, if a less one morally, than he had left it. He had turned his visit to Portugal to his own account, and so ingratiated himself with the Regent and the Infanta by his affectation of sanctity and professed belief in all that was of the Church of Rome, that they had sent him back with honour to his bishopric, thus recognising his ordination by the Babylonish patriarch. However, there is reason to believe that Mar Joseph was really in a great measure Romanised before his involuntary visit to Europe. The heads of the Syrian Church in the sixteenth century appear to have been, with few exceptions, distinguished for unfaithfulness, moral cowardice, and ambition, which made them ready, on their first contact with Rome, to sell the liberties of their people for a personal consideration. Thus Mar Joseph is said to have been in the habit of visiting the Portuguese at Cochin in order to earn from them the character of a good Catholic, and at the same time to have warned certain youths, whom the latter had introduced to him to be spies upon his conduct, against the favourite Romish doctrine that Mary was the mother of God. This duplicity, instead of strengthening his position, was the first cause of his troubles. It must have weakened his influence over the worthier members of his own church, and it made the opportunity which the Portuguese were seeking against him. Yet this man was not the first in his office who trod this path of shame. In 1549, Xavier wrote to the king of Portugal in the following terms about one who was probably the immediate predecessor of Mar Joseph— "For forty-five years a certain Armenian bishop, Jacob Abuna by name, has served God and your majesty. He is a man equally dear to God on account of his virtue and his sanctity, yet despised and neglected by your majesty, and by all who have any power in India. God has himself provided for his welfare. He regards us as unworthy of the honour of being employed as instruments for the consolation of his servant. The fathers of the order of St. Francis alone take care of him, and surround him with benevolent attentions which leave nothing wanting. . . . . This man is most worthy of the character I give him, because he spares no labour in ministering to the Christians of St. Thomas; and now, in his decrepid age, he most obediently accommodates himself to all the rites and customs of the Church of Rome." But, however such converts satisfied Xavier, they did not find it so easy to satisfy Don Juan d'Albuquerque; and in spite of the royal favours and compliments with which Mar Joseph returned to India, the bishop of Goa denounced him as a hypocrite to his face. Yet he allowed him to return to his diocese for good strategical reasons. Wily as the Syrians might be, Rome was sure to play the deeper game, and to win at last if wits decided the contest. Mar Joseph got a triumph when his enemies intended his ruin, but that being done they had the skill to make his triumph more useful to themselves than his ruin at that time would have been. It was thus that Don Juan sent him back to his diocese, because he knew that another was there before him, and that the two rival bishops would fight Rome's battle each against the other. The Syrians, dependent for everything upon their civil and ecclesiastical rulers, as the Jesuits had observed, and despairing of Mar Joseph's return, had sought another

Marginal notes:

An early example of Syrian conformity to Rome.

Reception and treatment of Mar Joseph by Don Juan d'Albuquerque.

Schism in the Syrian Church.

bishop from their patriarch at Babylon, and one named
Abraham had been consecrated and sent to fill the
vacant see. When Mar Joseph returned, Mar Abraham
was in his place, and neither had any inclination to
retire. A schism was the necessary result. Most of the
Syrians stood by the new prelate, because he was as yet
unconnected with Rome. But power at any price was
the motto of these men, and their eager-　**Mar Joseph**
ness to obtain it was, as usual, in inverse　**applies to the**
proportion to their worthiness. The weaker　**Portuguese**
applied to the Portuguese for help—to the　**for help.**
men who had seized his person that they might ruin his
church. The Portuguese were quite willing to accept
Mar Joseph as their tool, and at once laid their hands to
the work. His rival was put out of the
way, as he had been formerly—sent on a　**Mar Abraham**
compulsory voyage to Europe. But in　**transported.**
the accidents of a storm he managed to escape at
Mozambique, and to make his way to Mosul, where his
patriarch confirmed his title as bishop of Malabar.
However, he knew by this time that no Babylonian
credentials would command respect from Romish ecclesiastics, and he did not know what it was to put his
trust in God ; so he thought that the best　**He goes to**
stroke of worldly wisdom was to go to　**Rome and**
Rome, submit to the Pope, and receive　**submits to the**
the bishopric from his hands on the terms　**Pope.**
which he should dictate. Pius V. was a stern pontiff,
and his terms were hard for Mar Abraham. To anyone
who had not sacrificed faith and truth to policy they
would have been unbearable. He required the Syrian
bishop to abjure his ancient creed and to submit to
Roman ordination as the conditions of regaining his
diocese. As Mar Abraham thought more　**Mar Abraham**
of being a bishop than of being a Christian,　**returns to**
and these were the Pope's terms, he was　**India**
soon on his way to India with Papal　**with Papal**
authority. Before he arrived there his　**authority.**

rival was gone. Duplicity had deceived him. Thinking himself safe in Malabar he had broken his vows to the court of Portugal and resumed Syrian ways, so the Portuguese seized him a second time, and had him transported to Rome. What became of him there we are not told; but it is easy to imagine, when we remember that the reigning pope was a bigoted and blood-thirsty persecutor, a friend of the Inquisition, and the man who forbade the soldiers of the king of France ever to spare the life of a Huguenot prisoner.

The last of Mar Joseph.

Mar Joseph being finally removed, Mar Abraham might naturally have expected to take quiet possession of the diocese. But the Jesuits and their allies in India were determined to get rid of Syrian bishops, and therefore the authority of the pope availed no more than that of the patriarch of Babylon, and both together were insufficient to keep Mar Abraham out of a Portuguese prison. Thus again events were telling the Syrians the vanity of deceit, and their bishop, in the hands of his persecutors, had time to reflect on his journey to Rome, where he had sold his conscience and his character for—nothing. However, he managed to escape, as he had done at Mozambique, and was soon in the midst of his people. There he followed in the footsteps of his predecessors, trying to please all and pleasing none, re-ordaining his priests according to the ritual of Rome, and returning as much as he dared to the doctrines and customs of Syria. The Portuguese were of course enraged, and eager again to lay hold upon him, but he had been twice in their hands, and had learnt to keep out of them. He ventured, notwithstanding, to attend a council at Goa, on receiving a summons from the pope with letters of safe conduct. There, with characteristic facility he promised everything that was required of him, and with characteristic faithlessness, did nothing when he returned home

Mar Abraham put in prison.

He escapes, and behaves like his predecessors.

except to hold another Romish ordination. This it
would be natural for him to do in self-justification, since
he had submitted to papal ordination while at Rome.
At the same time he wrote to the Chaldean patriarch to
assure him that he remained true at heart to the ancient
church of Babylon. The weight of years and the
anxieties of his position pressing heavily upon him, Mar
Abraham, some time after this, begged from the
patriarch an assistant, who, in case of his death, might
succeed him in the diocese. His wish was granted, but
he soon found that he had asked for trouble to himself,
and his church. The days of the feud   The schism
with Mar Joseph were revived. The   in the church
assistant set himself up as independent   renewed.
bishop; the church was again split in two, and the new
and the old prelates anathematised one another, while
the Portuguese, and the Jesuits especially, looked on
with satisfaction to see their enemies so earnestly doing
their work. Mar Abraham, finding himself the weaker
of the two, called in the aid of the Europeans, who were
always as willing to sell their services as he was to sell
himself. They had become adepts at bishop catching,
and now for the fourth time they tried it with success.
The younger prelate, Simeon, was persuaded by the
Franciscans to do as Abraham had done,
and seek the patronage of the pope; but   Mar Simeon
fate mocked his folly by giving him the   disposed of.
voyage as a prisoner, and leaving him an exile for life
in the hands of the men he had unworthily courted.
Neither the pope, nor the inquisitors at Lisbon, tell us
what they did with Mar Simeon. But if the Portuguese
relieved Abraham of his rival's presence, it was only that
they might be nearer to their object of depriving the
Syrian church of its native leaders, since they reasonably expected that death would soon do their work with
the aged survivor. The schism, too, which was in their
favour, was kept open by the opposition of Simeon's
vicar-general Jacob, a valuable man to the Portuguese,

though an enemy, since he had influence **A new rival** enough to divide the church without that **to Abraham.** episcopal authority which it was their great aim to destroy. Had he been a bishop, and had his life been prolonged, this man would have given Rome trouble, for he seems to have been distinguished by something of the courage and uprightness which were so lamentably wanting in all the four bishops who have passed before us. The ecclesiastics of Goa made one more attempt, in 1590, to get the old prelate into their hands, inviting or summoning him to a council of their church, but he would not be charmed, and, as age soon after confined him altogether to his house, they had to allow him to spend the remainder of his days in peace, and in the open profession of the Syrian faith.

A more formidable enemy to the Syrian **Arrival in** Church than any which had yet assailed **India of** her was at this time buckling on his **Don Alexis** armour, and getting ready for a Romish **de Menezes.** crusade. This was Don Alexis de Menezes, archbishop elect of Goa. His orders from the pope were to examine into Mar Abraham's conduct, and if he found him guilty, that is, found him Syrian and not Romish, to seize him, and appoint a governor or vicar-apostolic of the Roman communion to administer the affairs of the diocese. Menezes was a distinguished Romanist, for his zeal out-shone that of the pope. He condemned the Syrian prelate at once; but the old man had now **Death of** to give in his account to a higher tribunal **Mar Abraham.** than that of Portugal, and he died in his bed, unaffected by the anathemas of Rome. His rival, Jacob, had died a little while before, so that Menezes had an easier work as well as greater talent than those who had gone before him. The prospects of the Syrians were then dark indeed, for the pope had given orders, which were faithfully executed, to prevent any communication of the Chaldean patriarch with the church of Malabar. Menezes nominated a Jesuit to the bishopric,

but the governor and council at Goa, who knew better
than the archbishop the character which the Jesuits had
earned in India, would not confirm the appointment.
The leading man among the Syrians was now the archdeacon George; and it was deemed the best policy to
get him to accept confirmation in his office by papal
authority. A joint commission with Romish ecclesiastics
was first offered him, and on his refusal of this, Menezes
proposed to him to retain the sole charge of his church,
after subscribing to the articles of the Romish faith.

We have now another Syrian leader
before us, and we naturally turn with
pleasure from the consideration of his
unworthy predecessors, hoping for better things in the
new character which the history introduces to us. But
all is again disappointment. If experience teaches the
foolish, the Syrian leaders were worse than foolish, for
they learnt nothing by experience, and archdeacon
George, with the failures of Joseph and Simeon and
Abraham before him, prepared to resume the battle with
those weapons of dissimulation which Rome knew how
to use so much better than any of her enemies. It is
sad to see a church bearing such a character as that of
Malabar—its members simple, honourable, generous,
even by the reports of their persecutors—represented by
men who are unworthy to be reckoned Christians at all.
But, as we have already noticed, there
was great weakness in the churches of
the East. A conservatism unknown in
Europe had preserved among them the
profession of much primitive doctrine, but the life was
for the most part gone; and while the recognition in
any way of pure Gospel morality may have been
sufficient to make the homely lives of the Syrians a
pattern to the surrounding heathen, it was not enough
to fit their leaders for discharging the duties and over-
coming the temptations of the episcopate in those days
of cruel, deceitful, and patronising Popery. It ought

also to be noticed, that the Syrian bishops were probably
in many cases strangers to India until they entered
upon their office. This seems, at any rate, to have been
the case with Abraham and Simeon, whom the Chaldean
patriarch sent out at the request of the Syrians; and if
so, the character of these men reflects dishonour, not
upon the church which suffered from their misconduct,
but upon the patriarch who could entrust the sacred
office of a bishop to such unworthy hands. This fact
removes much of the disgrace which at first appears
ineffaceable from the character of Malabar Christianity;
but much remains which we cannot remove. We have
no reason to doubt that archdeacon George was a Syrian,
and throughout the further history of Rome's aggressions
there are so many examples of shallowness and vacil-
lation in the mass of the people, and such a constant
absence of anything like spirituality of mind, or of the
truth held in the power of faith, as to make it quite
natural that the champion of the Church should be a
man not of spiritual power but of worldly policy. This
worldly policy decided the archdeacon to   Temporizing
temporize with Menezes, and to promise   policy of the
to do all he required at a certain time.   archdeacon.
When the time came he broke his word, as he had all
along intended to do. But Menezes was not a man to
be trifled with, and the archdeacon trembled as he
threatened to visit the Serra. He therefore offered to
subscribe to the Romish articles before any one but a
Jesuit. The Jesuits were disgusted, but Menezes took
him at his word, and appointed a Franciscan to hear his
confession. The confession, however, when   His unmeaning
it was extorted, was found to mean nothing,   confessions.
and the archdeacon was compelled to
make another before certain other monks of the same
order. But if on the former occasion he knew that his
confession meant nothing, on the latter he comforted
himself and explained to his people that he knew
nothing of what it meant. He had simply put his name

to a paper written in Portuguese, of which language he
was happy to be ignorant. After this attempt to satisfy
the Romanists, the archdeacon continued to preach as a
Nestorian. But he did not know the man he had to
deal with. Menezes was soon in his territories, pushing
the battle to the gate. A terrible man was this new
archbishop, with one strong arm for the Church and
another for the State ; zealous and crafty, bold and yet
cautious ; equally at home in treating with kings, out-
witting the archdeacon, bullying his priests, and deceiving
his people ; in all things worthy to have been a general
of the Jesuits. He intended no hasty   Menezes'
raid upon the Serra, but a visitation   intentions in
which should make him master of the   visiting the
country ; not of the person of the chief   Serra.
offender, for that, however it might have satisfied his
predecessors, would have been little to Menezes, but of
the churches and of the whole population. This was no
easy task ; for though the Syrian bishops had shown
themselves faithless, the mass of the people had no
motive for changing their religious opinions, and had
stoutly resisted the Franciscans and Jesuits who had
laboured to make them do so. But the Archbishop,
knowing his powers, not only undertook this difficult
task, but filled his hand with politics too, and showed
himself as skilful in plotting against hostile or friendly
rajahs for the aggrandisement of Portugal as he was in
proselytising among the simple but obstinate Syrians.
He commenced his visitation at Cannanore, and proceeded
thence to Cochin, where he was met by the terrified
archdeacon. But archdeacon George looked strong as
yet, for a numerous band of Syrian soldiers protected
him, and their captains swore to resist the designs of
Menezes. The archbispop betook himself   He preaches
to preaching, in which he must have had   in Portuguese.
singular faith, since the people are said
not to have understood a word of his speech. Still, a
Romish archbishop in his canonicals was an imposing

sight, and Menezes had at least as much hope of converting the people by their eyes as by their ears ; and,
no doubt, there were some who were able to tell the
unlearned afterwards how the archbishop had been
exposing the errors of Nestorianism, and proving the
claims of the Church of Rome.

The Syrians were a people remarkable for civility,
and while Menezes refrained from abuse they would
listen to him, or at least look at him with respect, and
many even submitted to be confirmed, Confirms some
having been sufficiently prepared for the of the Syrians
rite, according to Romish judgment, by a and gains two
"procession for sins." But little was ecclesiastics.
really gained as yet, excepting two Syrian ecclesiastics.
The people generally remained unconvinced, even when
they allowed the hands of Rome to be laid upon them,
and the violence of Menezes in denouncing their
patriarch at Babylon, excited their anger and put him
in some danger from the more warlike Syrians, while
the naires, or Hindu soldiery, against whose idolatry he
inveighed with equal boldness, were naturally offended
by the overbearing demeanour of the foreign priest.
Aware, however, that Hindus and Syrian christians
would mutter long before they would strike a blow at
the representative of Portugal, Menezes went on his
way, getting wiser and more formidable by experience.

Half a dozen places had been visited with these
results, when the archbishop had a conference with
archdeacon George, at which it was deter- Confers with
mined to hold a synod, for the settlement the archdeacon,
of all vexed questions, and to refrain, in and proposes
the meantime, from speaking or acting to hold a
against each other. This was such a truce
as the church of Rome has often resorted to—one by
which she has no intention of being bound herself,
seeing it is unnecessary to keep faith with heretics, but
by which she hopes to tie the hands of her opponents,
who may reasonably be expected to have more conscience

than herself. The archbishop and the archdeacon parted,
the latter to do nothing, the former to conduct important political arrangements, to plan the destruction of a
fort being built by a friendly native prince, to proclaim
a victory on the defeat of his countrymen, and to break
his faith with the Syrians on the earliest convenient
opportunity.

Fear of Menezes had hitherto re-
strained archdeacon George from open
hostility. He had hoped against hope,
and tried hard to believe some of the
promises of his adversary. He would
have purchased peace at any price but the absolute
subjection of his church to Rome; but that was
Menezes's only price, and the archdeacon was now forced
to see it, and to accept the only position that was left
him. He warned his people and the native princes of
the common danger, and called upon them to thwart the
Romish prelate. The Rajah of Cochin did what he
could, but he was too late. Menezes held
an ordination at Diamper, and so attached
thirty-eight priests to himself and the
cause of Rome. Thence he moved to
Carturté, a place of considerable importance, where even
greater success attended him. Threatened on his way
by the naires, insulted by the Christians, ordered out of
the district by the native ruler, he quietly worked on
with his many tools until Carturté gave
in its submission and was duly Romanised.
To produce such a result the archbishop
had to use all his talent. The naires were braved or
avoided; the ranee treated with, cajoled and outwitted;
the Syrians plied with every means by which the church
of Rome makes converts. The authority of Menezes
with his own church and countrymen, and consequent
power to promote those who espoused his cause, would
doubtless determine some to join him. Two at least,
already inclined that way, were gained by money and

Marginal notes:

Archdeacon George being deceived, breaks off communication.

First ordination of Syrians by Menezes.

Conquest of the church at Carturte.

promises, while the people in general were tempted by music, displays of dress, and similar appeals to their senses. At first this pomp, contrasting with their own simple worship, offended the Syrians; but it was too pleasing to human nature to continue to do so with men who had but little spiritual life, and so it worked as Menezes expected it to work, and gaining a place for itself, it introduced the teaching and the ceremonies which the Romish prelate blended with it, until the poor Syrians, who were confident of their stability as Peter, were the humble servants of their church's enemy, and ready to listen quietly to his proposal of deposing their archdeacon. The means by which the archbishop completed his victory at Carturté was the affectation of extraordinary humility and virtue. He washed the feet of the cattanars or Syrian priests, visited the sick throughout the town, and dispensed alms liberally, expressing abhorrence of the "simony" of the cattanars in receiving salaries from the people. The Syrians, of course, knew nothing of the archbishop's salary, and they were overwhelmed with admiration of his dis_ interestedness. He utilised his success by holding another ordination, and thereby in- increasing the number of his Romish Syrian priests. *Another Romish ordination.* Having learned to convert the people, Menezes' chief business lay in managing the native princes, who had become alarmed at his success, and were striving to hinder him. This was no difficult matter to a man of his spirit, *Menezes overawes the native princes.* backed by the authority of Portugal. The rajah of Cochin, who was the chief offender, and who had imprisoned, his subjects for giving a welcome to Menezes, was forced into an alliance, and the two shepherds— heathen king and Romish archbishop— drove the flocks of Molandurté and Diamper into the fold of the "catholic church." *Molandurté and Diamper subdued.* These three places being im-

portant centres, others of course quickly followed their
example: were baptised and confirmed, instructed in
the use of holy oils, the pix of the host, and other
matters of equal importance, and made to see the errors
of their ancient creed, the usurpation of their patriarch
at Babylon, and the truth and authority of the church of
Rome. Some points of Menezes' teaching, however, we
do not wonder that they were slow to   Objection of
receive. Auricular confession was es-   the Syrians
pecially unpalatable. But Menezes knew   to auricular
how to to affect forbearance, and he could   confession.
afford to wait for entire conformity in so tractable a
church. He even bore with the archdeacon, whom he
had intended at Carturté to depose at once. The
proselytes had begged twenty days' grace for the leader
they were deserting. Menezes, whose mask then was
that of an angel of light, did more than they desired,
and completed his visits to several other towns before he
again threatened the archdeacon. The latter, forsaken
by his own people, and a prey to increasing terror, at
length offered to submit. Menezes gave him ten articles
to sign, and twenty days in which to return them, with
the abjuration of his Syrian faith. The archdeacon
professed his readiness to do everything he was told,
but complained of the shortness of the time. His
persecutor saw that he was still leaning upon two
heathen princes, the rajahs of Cochin and Mangate.
Portuguese threats soon struck these props from under
him, and the Syrian fell into the arms of
the Roman Catholic. He signed away his   The archdeacon
faith and his liberty privately in the   finally submits.
Jesuit college of Vaipicotta.

A great part of the work which Rome had at heart
was now accomplished. What Franciscans and even
Jesuits had failed to do in many years of sapping and
mining, the new archbishop had effected by a bold
assault. His immense secular and ecclesiastical power,
and the force and subtility of his character, had made

him master of the Syrian archdeacon, and of many of the
Syrian churches. But the work wanted consolidating:
Menezes could not give his whole time to forging chains
for the people of Malabar; it was necessary that they
should learn to make them for themselves and to put
them on one another. He therefore returned to his
early proposal of holding a synod, at which   Renewed
the doctrines and practices of the church   proposal of
of Malabar should be considered and   a general
determined. No one who heard this   synod.
proposal could have the slightest doubt what it meant.
The man who had laboured so earnestly to establish the
dominion of the pope in Malabar, could have no thought
of allowing his captives to think for themselves. Yet a
synod was a good thing in itself. Many of the churches
were now fascinated by Menezes, the rest were terrified
and disunited, and the archdeacon had surrendered at
discretion. So the synod was easily arranged. The
place chosen was Diamper, already famous for the
ordination of Menezes' first company of
Syro-Romish priests. The archbishop   It is held at
called together the clergy whom he had   Diamper.
proselytised, and the archdeacon, at the command of his
master, summoned the rest of the Cattanars. Six weeks
intervened between the invitations and the opening of
the synod—six weeks which offered one more opportunity
to the Christians of Malabar to consider their position;
and to avert the ecclesiastical destruction which
threatened them. But as in every former case, the
opportunity was lost. The church was paralysed if it
was not dead. There was no effort, no consultation, no
prayer. In this state of helplessness and spiritual
unconsciousness they went to meet their enemies at
Diamper.

But if the six weeks were nothing to the   Menezes'
Syrians, they were much to Menezes and   preparation for
his church. By the assistance of Francis   the synod.
Roz, an able Jesuit, and an accomplished Syrian scholar,

G

he drew up the decrees for the approaching synod, arranging what the Syrians were henceforth to do and believe, and consecrated a stone altar for every one of their churches in Malabar. But most important of all, lest any reaction among his recent proselytes should make it possible he should be found in a minority, he added fifty priests to the number he had already ordained on the abjuration of their ancient creed, gave bribes freely, and laboured in correspondence both with the Portuguese and with the native rajahs to remove every misunderstanding and every political hindrance which might affect the completeness of his success. The result was worthy of Menezes, and worthy of the Syrians. God was not in the matter on either side, as far as the testimony of history goes. There was purpose, union, and craft on the one side; apathy, disorder, and infatuation on the other. Rome, of course, triumphed. Those who are acquainted with her invasion of the Church of Britain in the seventh century, and who know how she bore down all before her in spite of the piety and heroism of hundreds of our native clergy, will not wonder at her easy conquest of Malabar.

The synod of Diamper met on the 20th of June, 1599, and on the 26th it had settled the affairs of the Syrian Church. Considering the extent of its decrees, and the prodigious number of doctrines and practices which it corrected or introduced, business appears to have been got through. very quickly ; a circumstance not very remarkable when it is remembered that the real council had been sitting for six weeks in Menezes' cabinet, and that there was scarcely any faith, ability, or courage among the Syrians to oppose or even to question the decrees which the archbishop and his Jesuit colleague had prepared for their reception. If we may suppose the synod of Diamper to have represented the Syrian Church, and by their submission, obedience to the summons, and failure to make any protest, *The Syrian Church united by the synod of Diamper to that of Rome.*

both the archdeacon and his clergy allowed this to be
the case, that ancient church was thus legally united to
Rome, and perverted to all the superstitions and idolatries
of popery. No doubt there were many towns and
villages in the Serra where Menezes and his doctrines
were still held in abhorrence; many he had, probably,
never visited, and some few had resisted him successfully;
but the only native head of the church, and its representatives in the leading cities, had, through infatuation
or cowardice, sold the liberties of all in subscribing the
decrees of the synod of Diamper. Henceforth the pope
and his warlike legate might rest from the labours of
invasion, and devote their energies to the easier task of
holding and governing a conquered people.

The activity of Menezes was not
diminished by the success of the synod. *Menezes*
He set out to apply that success by a *revisits the*
second visitation of the Serra—not this *and applies the*
time as the foreign ecclesiastic with unac- *Decrees of*
knowledged claims, but as the Catholic *the synod.*
archbishop of Goa, and metropolitan of the Syrian
Churches. Where he was received before, he was not
likely to be resisted now; consequently his progress had
often the appearance of a triumphal procession. Indeed,
on the occasion of his arrival at the episcopal city of
Angamale, his reception is said to have been arranged
after the model of our Lord's last public entry into
Jerusalem. Notwithstanding this recognition of the
dignity of Angamale, Menezes decreed that it should
cease to be the residence of the Syrian bishop, and that
Cranganore, which was more easily reached by the
influences of Goa, should be the episcopal city. As he
passed from place to place, he not only, as apostles had
once done, "delivered them the decrees for to keep," but
he added what apostles did not, and enforced the keeping
of them with a strong arm of flesh. Everybody at
Diamper, and probably in other places also, was re-
baptised. The Cattanars were forced to separate from

their wives; the people were confirmed and urged to the
use of auricular confession, against which, as well as
against confirmation, they still showed much of their
original repugnance. All books in the **Destroys**
Syriac language were called for, that they **many of the**
might be corrected according to the synod, **Syrian books.**
or destroyed. From the extreme fewness of such books
now in existence, it is reasonably supposed that this
demand of Menezes was as fully complied with as the
rest, and that the eye of the bigoted Romanist found
the books of the ancient and independent church too
free from the errors of his own corrupted faith, and too
much in agreement with primitive and scriptural truth,
to allow many of them to escape destruction. Thus this
able and devoted servant of Rome afforded another of
those many proofs which history keeps on record, that
she is ready to destroy all knowledge, secular and sacred,
in order to prolong or extend her reign of darkness over
the minds of men.

At the close of his second visit to the
Serra, Menezes appointed the humbled and **The**
powerless archdeacon to a nominal share of **Archdeacon**
authority in his church, associating him **appointed to a**
with two Jesuits, the rector of the College **nominal and**
at Vaipicotta and Francis Roz. This **temporary authority.**
arrangement, however, was only to last until the people
were persuaded to choose a Latin bishop, and being now
Romanised themselves they were not slow to accede to
the proposal. They first wanted Menezes himself to be
their bishop, but he had higher honours in his church
than that of bishop of the Serra, though he affected a
readiness to resign all for the joy and privilege of tending
the flock whom he had brought into the Catholic fold.
The man who had most helped him in this work was
Francis Roz, and him they selected for their bishop.
Menezes left the work in the hands of this able lieutenant
and returned to Goa to reap the reward of his labours.
He was made Viceroy of India; and, armed with all the

secular authority of Portugal and all the ecclesiastical authority of Rome, he continued to labour by force and fraud for the glorification of his church and himself.

But this point touches the strict limit of our subject. Beyond it we pass into the seventeenth century. We must very briefly sketch the history of the Syrians after this time. Before doing so, however, we cannot but take a parting glance at the man who had destroyed their liberties. *The last of Don Alexis de Menezes.* He was another Wolsey—another example of successful fraud, and late but heavy retribution. He returned to Europe, rose to the highest offices of the state, then fell, and died in obscurity; so complete being his disgrace that history scarcely pauses to tell the end of the man who had decided the fate of one of the most ancient churches of Christendom. We know that this life is not the time in which men reap their full reward; but we cannot take this last look of Don Alexis de Menezes, Archbishop of Goa, and Viceroy of India, without recalling the words of Paul to Timothy :—" Some men's sins are open before hand, going before unto judgment."

Francis Roz was consecrated in 1601, and ruled the Syrians for sixteen years, leaving the office to other Jesuits, who completed the work which Roz had begun, and by pride, selfishness, and cruelty, *The rule and influence of Jesuit bishops over the Syrian Church.* taught the poor Syrians, whom they treated as slaves, to understand the character of the Church whose yoke they had put upon their own necks. For sixty years they learned their bitter lessons in the school of experience, showing how slowly they apprehended the truth by their frequent appeals to Rome for deliverance. But at last they seem to have found out that their masters were the pope's masters too, and they declared themselves again independent. They rallied under their archdeacon, but sent to Mosul, to Syria, and to Egypt for a bishop. The *The Syrians rebel after sixty years of oppression.* patriarch at Mosul readily acceded to their request, but

the bishop whom he sent was captured, and after a time
of imprisonment, from which the Syrians vainly attempted to rescue him, was murdered by the Inquisition.
This crime, like most crimes, directly hindered the cause
it was intended to promote. The Syrians, still divided
and irresolute, needed a stimulant in their resistance;
the murder of Attala afforded it, and refreshed their
memories regarding the true character of the Jesuits in
particular. But a subtle attack of a similar kind to that
of Menezes' was more than they were able to meet.
Four Carmelites set out from Rome to
bring back the wanderers. Two arrived
long before the others, and laboured with
a good deal of skill and success to quell
the insurrection. They were not Jesuits:
An expedition of Carmelites is sent from Rome to reclaim them.
that made them popular with many; for the churches
of the South had revolted, not from Rome, but from
their Jesuit bishops. But they were thwarted by the
hated Order, who cared not what they sacrificed so long
as they did not sacrifice themselves. Moreover,
Portuguese influence could help them little; for the
sun of Portugal was setting, and the Dutch, with their
republican courage and Protestantism, were driving
them from one stronghold after another.

Yet the feeble Syrians, who, in less favourable circumstances, would have yielded everything, and whom
Menezes would have trampled on in a few weeks, were
for the most part won by the wiles of the Carmelites,
who were greatly inferior in subtlety to the first
conqueror. The result of many negociations, interrupted
conferences, and proposals on either side,
was that a great number of the Syrian
churches returned to their allegiance to
Rome, and accepted one of the Carmelites
The south of the Serra again submits to Rome.
as their bishop. Those which did so were in the
southern and wealthier division of the Serra; the
churches of the north retained the independence they
had resumed. But the new bishop harassed them inces-

santly, and by means of money, patronage, heathen rajahs, and heathen soldiers, drove the free Syrians from many of their churches. He very nearly succeeded in capturing the archdeacon, and having seized his effects he burned some of them, expressing his regret that it was not the rebel's body he was committing to the flames. The capture of Cochin by the Dutch, in 1663, checked his progress ; for the Dutch drove all priests before them, and refused to allow them to return even in time of peace. This determined the Romish bishop to retire to Europe, but he had previously consecrated a native suffragan, whom he left to supply his place. The Dutch did nothing directly for the free Syrians, but even showed a preference for the Romish party, being deceived by the misrepresentations of the Carmelite bishop. Their arrival, however, was the termination of persecution and active hostilities. From that time the Serra was divided between two churches, national and Romish, bitterly opposed to one another, although they had groaned together under sixty years of Jesuit oppression. The archdeacon, whom his priests had ordained as bishop during the imprisonment of Attala, and the Syrian whom the Carmelites had set over the Southern churches, died about the same time. After this the Northern churches seem to have been for some time without a head : possibly the temporary freedom of the South from Jesuit bishops caused them to relax something of their zeal for independence. In 1708, they are said to have received a Nestorian bishop from Syria, and this agrees well with the fact that the South, after being governed by natives under Carmelite influence, fell again into the hands of the Jesuits in 1701. The last link of this period which we possess in the chain of Romish bishops, is the accession of another Jesuit to the

Marginal notes:

Persecution of the free Syrians by the Carmelite bishop.

Open persecution checked by the arrival of the Dutch.

Deaths of the Northern and Southern bishops.

The Jesuits again in the episcopate.

episcopal office in 1721. We do not wonder if the return of their old tyrants and persecutors increased the distance between the free and the Romanized Syrians. And thus the breach in the ancient Church of Malabar, which was made a thousand years ago by the pride of wealth and birth, has been kept open to the present time.

The ancient breach in the Church perpetuated.

No doubt it tended much, in the first days of Romish aggression, to make all the Serra an easy prey to Menezes, and so to bring the whole church under the severe chastisement which we have been briefly describing. But it is interesting to observe that the last result of that separation which the South had forced upon the North, in an unchanging spirit of contempt, and so in utter and continued

Pride and destruction illustrated in the fate of the South.

neglect of Christian love, was the relighting of the candle of truth among the despised ones, while their proud brethren of the South remained for the most part in the darkness of Popery. As to the latter, suffering and trial did not, as they have often done, impart strength to their character or develope latent good. They had pure doctrine, but having no spiritual life or moral courage to maintain it, what they had was almost entirely taken away. Their light was put out, and when the extreme pressure of the dark power of Portugal was gone, they cared not and knew not how to rekindle it.

But although history says nothing, excepting in the matter of the pride of the south, to make us prefer the northern Syrians, or expect better things from them than from their brethren, they do seem to

Some little advantage reaped by the North from its troubles.

have learnt something by the time of trouble. The account which Dr. Buchanan gives of them from his visit in 1806, represents a better state of things in some of the clergy than appears to have obtained in the time of Menezes'

Different opinions about the state of the clergy.

invasion. The portrait of the bishop especially, affords

a pleasing contrast to those which the history of the
sixteenth century has laid before us. It is that of "a
man of highly respectable character in his church';
eminent for his piety and for the attention he devotes to
his sacred functions," and far superior in general
learning to his clergy, although these, as far as Dr.
Buchanan had experience of them, appear as intelligent
and religious men. We must notice, however, that the
impression made upon the mind of another church of
England clergyman, who visited them twelve years later,
was much less favourable, and that whatever exceptions
there may have been, the general character of the clergy
appeared to him to be very low. He speaks of the
people as "sunk and degraded indeed," and adds, "the
total disregard of the Sabbath, the profanation of the
name of God, drunkenness, and to a considerable extent,
especially among the priesthood, adultery, are very
prevalent among them." Sorrows besides those which
Rome had caused them had broken the spirit of the
nation. The rajah of Travancore had conquered their
country, and cruelly oppressed them; and the result
seems to have been an increase of moral weakness
and the diminishing of self-respect and of hope. Still,
they were by no means hopeless to those who described
them thus; for these true friends, who could estimate
most correctly the degradation, set themselves earnestly
to raise them up.

A mission of the church of England
was established among them in 1815,
through the exertions of Major Munro,
the Christian and philanthropic resident
at Travancore. By his means four clergymen of intelligence and piety were settled among the
Syrians, one at Allepie and three at Cotym.
The head quarters of the mission were at
the latter place, and there a college was
founded for the education of Syrian youths.
The machinery was much the same as

The Church
Missionary
Society in
Malabar.

A College
and Schools
founded, and
the Scriptures
translated into
Malayalim.

that of the Franciscans and the Jesuits, but the motive
of the workers and the use which they made of it were
very different. All that these labourers of the Church
Missionary Society strove to do, was to bring back the
Church of Malabar to a spiritual acquaintance with its
ancient creed. One great means to this end was the
dispelling of the sloth and ignorance which had settled
upon the nation. The college and a number of schools,
established throughout the Serra, helped to do this. But
the missionaries, and some among the Syrians themselves,
felt that the great means must be the dissemination of
the Word of God. Dr. Buchanan, ten years before, had
exerted himself to procure this boon for them, and his
efforts were partially successful. The old bishop, whom
he describes, entered heartily into the work, and very
soon translated the four gospels into Malayalim, the
vernacular language of the people. But the work seems
to have stopped there for some years, as Mr. Bailey, the
superintendent of the college at Cotym, devoted himself
chiefly to the translation of the Scriptures, until he was
able to produce the first part of his work in 1826.

The Bible Society had presented the
Syrians with the Syriac New Testament in
1818, providing at least one copy for every
one of their churches; but this language
was now scarcely spoken by any but the priests, and
the great want of the people had to be supplied from the
press at Cotym. Besides this best of all services, and
the instruction of the Syrian youth, the English
missionaries were made the medium of all the kind
offices of the British government in the redress of
grievances, and the general protection of the people from
tyranny. And thus a most happy and
well-grounded confidence has been created
among this much abused people in the
Established Church and government of
India—a confidence which is not likely to fail in raising
the moral tone of the Syrians, and reflecting honour of

Syriac New Testament provided by the Bible Society.

Confidence of the Syrians in the English missionaries.

the truest kind upon the country whose statesmen and missionaries have befriended them.

More than once the desire has been expressed that this Protestant remnant of the Syrian Church might be united with the Established Church of England. Apparently the first to entertain this

Proposal of uniting the Syrian Church with that of England.

thought were the directors of the Society for the Promotion of Christian Knowledge, who were generously lending their aid to the Danish and German pioneers of Tranquebar. But the design was abandoned as impracticable at that time, owing to the low state in which the Syrians were found. No doubt some advantages might reasonably have been expected from this union, such as the protection and support of an aged and feeble church, and the prestige and authority of that church communicated to one that, with all its numbers and strength, would be regarded in the East as foreign and of comparatively recent existence. But on the other hand, we could scarcely see without regret a church of such antiquity and such a history as that of Malabar ceasing to possess a separate individuality. It would seem to us like the transference of some grand old Roman column from its lonely forum to the busy precincts of a modern palace. Let British power overshadow and preserve it. Let Christian charity delight to enrich it with the spiritual life and knowledge of the West, but let it remain a pillar of memorial, upon which the history of fifteen hundred years is written, an independent testimony against the Apostate Church of Rome, and a witness in the midst of the heathen to the chastening but protecting hand of God.

———

The close of the sixteenth century was the close of the first part of the missionary labours of Rome in India. Early in the

Later Romish Missions to the Heathen.

next century her emissaries introduced an entirely new
system for the conversion of the heathen. The details of
their labours do not belong to our present subject, but
we cannot leave them entirely unnoticed, as it is impossible to separate between the fruits of these late
missions and that of Xavier and his contemporaries in
considering the influence of Hindu Romanism on the
labours of Protestant missionaries.

We have already arrived at an estimate of the first
Romish missions to India in considering the impression
made by them upon the mind of Xavier. There was no
one more competent to judge correctly in this matter;
for Xavier, besides being the man of largest experience,
was on the one hand honest, intelligent, and christian at
heart, and on the other enthusiastic, sanguine, and
zealous for Rome. He would have believed in conversions if it had been possible to do so; but after
baptising tens of thousands, he left the country
dissappointed and heartsick, openly declaring that there
was no further need of his services, and advising his
sovereign to make the conversion of the heathen the
business of civil magistrates, that is, to be satisfied with
compelling Hindus to adopt the name and forms of the
religion of Rome, since her missionaries had no power
among them to change their hearts and lives. Xavier's
converts were all of the lowest caste, or of no caste, with
the exception of one Brahmin, who professed Christianity
in order to obtain employment; and, poor converts as they
were, few of them could be claimed by him, as the mass was
ready to be baptised when he reached the shores of
India. His biographers and his church generally gave
him credit for extraordinary success; but his wily
brethren the Jesuits, while they gloried in his fame, saw
that he had failed and sought to profit by his experience.
Xavier's simplicity, purity, and earnestness had been
thrown away upon the Brahmins, much as he had desired
to bring them within the fold of his church. His
successors determined to use other means for the same

purpose. The age of blind but often honest zeal was
followed by that of deliberate fraud. Xavier was the
representative of the first, Robert de Nobili of the second.
The latter entered upon his work about the   Jesuit
year 1606, in the city of Madura. By that   Brahmins and
time the Jesuits were, as we have seen, in   Brahminized
force and power in the East. De Nobili   christianity.
gave a new direction to their energies, and boldly
developing the peculiarities of Jesuitism in himself and,
his associates, he gave it a form which continued to
characterise the missionaries of the Society both in India
and China until the suppression of the order in 1773.
The zeal, the courage, the perseverance of the Jesuits had
before this been tried on many a field, and had sur-
mounted innumerable difficulties; but the Brahmins
of India were stubborn antagonists, and offered no hope.
to ordinary means of conversion. This showed the new
Jesuits that they must use extraordinary means; for
Jesuits must succeed at any cost and by any means
where success is possible. De Nobili and his associates,
sacrificed everything to their missionary object. Outside
the history of true Christianity there is no   Devotedness
record of more complete devotedness than   of these later
that of the Jesuits of Madura. All the   Jesuits.
ease and comforts of life were as thoroughly yielded up
as ever they have been by Protestant missionaries, or
even by primitive apostles. But more than this,
reputation and principle, the goodwill of their church,.
and even of their general, were all cast, like Palissy's last
furniture, into the flames, in the hope of producing the
one soul-absorbing object. Nothing was left but the.
proud indomitable self, which could sit in the midst of
the desolation, contented with the freedom of its own.
bad will. These later Jesuits presented themselves to
the heathen as heathen like themselves—Brahmins from,
another part of the world and of the very highest order.
They had previously studied the language and religion of.
the Hindus, in order to be able to maintain this.

character; and the learning and skill which they devoted to their life-long lie have never been surpassed in the cause of truth. By the most solemn asseverations respecting their Hindu origin, by forged documents, and by the adoption of idolatrous customs, they succeeded in establishing themselves among the natives in the character which they had assumed. They then proceeded to graft some of the doctrines of Roman Christianity upon the Hinduism which they professed, by inventing a book after the model of the most sacred Shastras, with texts of Scripture and fables of Rome cleverly interspersed among the sayings of Brahma, and introducing it to the Brahmins as the fifth Veda.

By these means, and by exclusive at- Converts
tention to the ruling caste and Brahminical to Brahminized
contempt for the lower orders, they soon Christianity.
met with some measure of success; and developing gradually the Romish element of their new religion, they led those who were deceived by them into a system which they declared to Europe to be Christianity, but which Rome, and even the popes of Rome, repudiated with a rarely felt sentiment of shame. But the Jesuits worked on steadily, in spite of Papal reprimands and condemnation, and the mission field was almost abandoned to them, for Franciscans and Carmelites could not stand against these skilful and determined rivals, with their Brahminical Christianity. Their head quarters were at Madura and Pondicherry, but they spread themselves throughout southern India, and sent their emissaries to the court of Akhbar, at Delhi; while others of their order laboured on the same principles and with like results among the Buddhists of China. For nearly one hundred and fifty years the fraud of de Nobili, and the still more learned and infamous Beschi, the great Indian Jesuit of the eighteenth century, remained undiscovered, and thousands of Hindus were led to its
worse than Romish Christianity. These, Numbers of
together with the political converts of Cape Romish Converts.

Comorin, and others who had rewarded the labours of earlier missionaries in South India, amounted in 1740 A.D. to about 245,000. But from that time, the great fraud having become known, conversions among the Brahmins ceased, and the statistics of the Hindu Romish Church dwindled in 1810 to about 81,000, or one-third of what they had been seventy years before.

Thus, even numerically, Romish missions to India must be considered a failure. And this appears more clearly when we consider the vast amount of authority, and wealth, and learning, and energy which has supported them for three hundred years. For a century and a half after their first establishment there was no Protestant mission on the con- *Immense amount of instrumentality* tinent of India. With papal and royal *to produce* powers their missionaries worked on with- *these numbers.* out a rival. Goa, the city of churches and monasteries, sent out its 3,000 priests and overawed with its dreadful Inquisition, not only the converts of Rome, but all who would tempt them to return to their ancient faith. What terror could do, that inquisition did. Founded in 1560, it blackened the soil of *The Inquisition in India.* India till 1816. According to the testimony of the traveller Pyrand, its cruelties were even greater than those perpetrated in Spain and Portugal, its executions more frequent, its dungeons more horrible, and the hopes of its captives more groundless. To aid in the work of this hideous tribunal, Catholic Europe laboured mightily, waking up in the beginning of the seventeenth century to an activity which she had never known before. From that time, "Congregations," "Colleges," "Seminaries" for the propagation of the faith sprang into existence both at Rome and in Paris, and vastly stimulated the work of proselytism. But in spite of them *Worthlessness of* all there was no great harvest of converts, *later Romish* and what was reaped has been declared by *Converts as well* honest Romanists, and proved by the facts *as of those of* of history to have been at least as worth- *Xavier.* less as the fruit of Xavier's mission.

The Abbé Dubois, an honest Jesuit, who for many
years, and with an earnestness which challenged the
scrutiny of his enemies, strove to make converts in
southern India, retired from the mission field in despair
in 1815. His settled conviction, after this long experience, and with a knowledge of the labours of his
predecessors and contemporaries, was that the conversion
of Hindu idolators was an impossibility. The result of
his own efforts had been the baptism of two or three
hundred outcasts, vagabonds, and slaves, not one of
whom could be reckoned a genuine convert, since many
of them returned to Paganism, while those who continued to call themselves Christians were in their lives
the worst of all. To establish his opinion
he published the fact—as he said, to his   Instance of
own shame, but surely much more to that   general apostacy.
of his Church—that of 60,000 native Romanists seized
in Mysore by the bigoted Mussulman, Tippoo Sultan,
with a view of extirpating Christianity by compelling
them to become Mahometans, not one was found who
had the faith and courage to prefer death for the sake of
Christ, to circumcision in the name of the false prophet.
From the miserable condition of the converts everywhere,
and the rapid decrease of their numbers, the Abbé
declared his conviction that within fifty years no vestige
of Christianity would remain among them. This result,
if it was at that time imminent, has been prevented by
a great increase of missionary effort within the Church
of Rome during the last forty years. India has felt
with Europe the result of the re-establishment of the
Jesuits in 1814. A new life—though by no means a
spiritual life—has been communicated to the missions of
Rome since they recovered possession of the field. But
if they succeed in restoring an appearance of numerical
strength they will not surpass Xavier in zeal, or De
Nobili and Beschi in learning or fraud ; and therefore,
having no new implements for the work, the most they
can expect to do is to reproduce the weary history of the

past three hundred years, and to continue to exhibit to the world a roll of meaningless baptisms, and a paganism and immorality under the Christian name, which must go far to prove to discerning minds, whether in Europe or in India, the spiritual impotence and antichristian character of their Church.

But the story of Protestant Indian missions is that which proves most clearly the failure of the missionaries of Rome. In contrast with the ecclesiastical authority *The contrast of Protestant with Romish Missions.* and the royal funds which supported Xavier and his successors, the Protestant missionaries on the mainland of India have had to struggle, in almost every instance, against com- *Difficulties which beset Protestantism.* parative poverty and the opposition or plainly expressed contempt of the government. It is true that in the first efforts of Protestantism by means of Ziegenbalg and Plutchou at Tranquebar, the hand of a king laid the foundation of the work, and an archbishop had something to do with building upon it. But the patronage of these dignitaries was a very different thing from the protection and stimulant which the Pope and a Roman Catholic king could lend to the work of Xavier or Menezes. It was not enough to protect the humble and uncomplaining preachers of the Gospel from the hostility of the Danish governor, or to prevent the continual recurrence of trial and difficulty through the scantiness of the means provided for their support. Moreover their numbers were not at any time to be compared with those engaged in Romish missions ; the difficulty of influencing the heathen at all had greatly increased since the days of Xavier, by reason of the shameless immorality which for two hundred years had been associated with Christianity; while the object of their labours was vastly greater and proportionately harder to attain than that which occupied the thoughts of the Jesuits, since it

H

was the turning of idolators to God and to holiness of life, and not merely the drawing of them to an earthly church and to a change of rites and ceremonies.

In spite, however, of these difficulties, **Unquestionable** men were found as ready as Xavier to **character of** undertake the work, and the results have **Protestant** shown that they did not over-rate their **missionaries** strength. Not that there has been no **in general.** failure among Protestant missionaries. Instances of eccentricity, want of wisdom, inconsistency, and even of immorality, have occurred, which have checked the progress of the work. But there is no honest person who knows anything of the history of these missions who would not readily acknowledge that such instances, particularly those of moral inconsistency, have been extremely rare, and that Protestant missionaries have often won a hearing for their doctrines by the blamelessness of their lives. Let any one who would know the force of their testimony read the life of Christian Frederick Schwartz, the man whom Hyder Ali— Mussulman and enemy of the British—called "the Christian," and who saved the fort of Tanjore from the fierce soldier who paid him this weighty compliment by an influence over the surrounding country which no Hindu prince, or British general was able to exercise And though Schwartz was a greater man **Example of** than most of his brethren, their religion **Schwartz.** was the same as his, and his life presents no contrast to theirs as that of Xavier does to the lives of other Romish missionaries. If Schwartz was "the Christian" to Hyder Ali, the elder Gerické was known **And the elder** as "the primitive Christian" by those **Gerické** among whom he had spent thirty-seven years of holy and self-denying labour; and the later history of Southern India abounds with examples of men who for thirty, forty, and even fifty years gave evidence that they were worthy to be associated with Schwartz and Gerické, as Christians and as missionaries.

We do not wonder, then, that in spite of such difficulties as never occurred to Xavier and his followers, particularly the infatuation of England at the beginning of the present century, in publicly patronizing idolatry and offering every possible obstacle to the preaching of the Gospel, the truth declared by the lips and the lives of these men has won its way where the superstitions of Popery have utterly failed. We do not wonder that Brahmins and men of learning and wealth have yielded to the power which has energized these missions, and that from among them and other grades of natives— Hindu, Mahometans, and Romanist—a class of men has arisen who have been worthy helpers and successors of the great Protestant pioneers of Germany, and who, having renounced the hidden things of dishonesty, have commended themselves to every man's conscience, in the sight of God, by many years of patiently endured suffering and effectual labour.

The reason of this difference between Romish and Protestant missions is easily told. The former were the efforts of man in his own will, his own wisdom, and his own power. But the task was too great for man, and so they failed. The latter were in great part the work of God; for a few weak men, conscious of their weakness, offered themselves to God for a work which strong men had been unable to do. They depended upon His Spirit, and spoke His Word, and suffered Him to work in their lives a manifestaion of His truth; and God used them, as they expected, to the conversion of many thousands in southern India. Moreover, the triumph of the simple Gospel in these first Protestant missions was enhanced not only by the greatness of the obstacles overcome, and the manifest reality of most of the converts who were gathered, but also by the successful assaults which were made upon the very strongholds of Hinduism. The high caste Hindus had hitherto been unreached by Christianity.

Reason of the different results of Romish and Protestant missions.

H 2

Xavier had no influence with them at all.
De Nobili and Beschi adopted Brahminism
that they might Romanize it, and the
success of their labours depended upon
leaving the pride and power of the ruling
caste untouched.

Influence of Protestant truth on some Hindus of the highest caste.

But the missionaries of Tranquebar,
although they made the mistake of allowing caste some
place in their Christian assemblies, and shrunk with unreasonable fear from ordaining to the ministry a low caste
native catechist, had nevertheless, in preaching the plain
Gospel of God, to insist upon those who would become
Christians taking up the cross and openly following the
rejected Saviour. So many were willing to do this,
moved by the power of truth alone, that Schwartz could
answer the mischievous calumny of an enemy in the
British Parliament by pointing to the fact that in three
native assemblies which he and his companions had
gathered, more than two-thirds of the converts were
Hindus of the higher castes ; and the
reality of the change in the members of
these Protestant churches was tested by
one example among many—which con-
trasts strikingly with the case of general
apostacy from Romanism which we have

Proof of the sincerity of Protestant converts by the persecution in Tinnevelly.

noticed on the authority of the Jesuit Dubois—when
the recently baptised Christians of Tinnevelly were tried
by a severe and general storm of persecution, and came
out of it without one of them having been known to
have denied his faith.

The sudden gathering of great numbers to the cross
has been rare in India as it has been elsewhere, though
it has happened in unquestionable instances both in the
South and North. But even while the
work has progressed most slowly, and all
but a few have rejected the testimony,
the workers have had the experience of
the Lord Himself in His ministry on
earth, and have realised what apostles

Protestant mis- sions have done all that Scrip- ture warrants N. T. mission- aries to expect.

rejoiced to realise in the early days of the dispensation of the Spirit, that God had by their hand visited the Gentiles "to take out of them a people for his name."

The direct and immediate effect of Romish missions upon the later labours of Protestants has been an increase of trouble. The slightest glance at the missionary history of the last hundred and sixty years puts this beyond a doubt. Not even the heathen, whose religion was directly invaded, were such constant and bitter enemies to the truth as those who had been baptised by Romish priests in the name of Christ. It was these "Christians" who stirred up the heathen, while their own energies were stimulated to the work of persecution by their unwearying priests. Father Beschi, of the Madura mission, does not more deserve to be remembered as the deceiver of Brahmins, and the perverter, *par excellence*, of Christian truth, than as the chief opponent and persecutor of the evangelists of India during many years of the eighteenth century. These facts, however, do not prevent us seeing that real good resulted to the servants of God in India through the presence of Romanists. "Tribulation worketh patience"—one of the rarest and, according to Scripture, one of the most precious fruits of the Spirit,—and the persecution by the Romanists which early Protestants in India had to suffer most certainly produced this result both in the pastors and their flocks; so that they had cause, through the grace and providence of God, not only to "rejoice in hope of glory," but "to glory in tribulation also," because of the blessings which it brought. But there were exceptions to this spirit of bigotry among the Romanised Hindus, doubtless where there was a lack of priests to produce it; and in some of these cases the slight inroad which Popery had made upon their original idolatries, and the name into which they had been baptised, made

The direct and indirect influence of Romanism upon evangelistic work in India.

Grace brought out by persecution.

the people ready to listen to the words of Hindu converts from Romanism. those who came to them as Christian missionaries. From this class many have been gathered into the church of Christ, and among them some of its most devoted and honoured labourers, as Rajanaiken and his brother Sinappius, who served together in the Gospel for forty-four years, and drew the well-known Sattianaden and many other Romanists to the knowledge of the truth. The priests Converted Romish priests. of Rome themselves, even her Jesuits and inquisitors, have not always been able to resist the weapons of the Gospel, and some of them have been turned on the soil of India to preach the faith which once they destroyed. Anxious ones Anxious ones helped by Romish agency in the search for truth. too among the heathen, awakened without any visible means to a knowledge of sin and a desire for salvation, have sometimes been led by Romish converts or Romish books to a study of Christianity which has resulted in their becoming fellow-labourers of the Protestant missionaries in the work of the Gospel.

Thus in a variety of ways God has shown that He could overrule the efforts of the apostate church to the building of His kingdom. But these are undoubtedly rare exceptions to the general influence of Romanism in India. In His moral government of the Closing reflections on the purpose of God in review of past history. world, God allows men much liberty of will and action, and therefore evil must have room to work. Evil did work, apparently unrestrained, in the persecution of the Church of Malabar, and in the Jesuit missions which made the name of Christ to be abhorred among the heathen. But the free will and depravity of man cannot tie the hands of God. He has His purposes of government and of grace to nations and to individuals. As one of the early fathers said, "God never works in a hurry, for He has got all eternity to work upon." No nation has been raised to Christian enlightenment and moral strength without a long preparation. Each has its infancy, growth, and full age, and these involve a school time of experience. While the darkness remains, and while it is rolling away with a slowness that provokes the impatience of unbelief, the Judge of all the earth must be just to all, and He will as surely acknowledge the gropings after truth that are unseen by man, as He will those efforts which in better times lead quickly to the light of the Gospel. But while thus the unwritten lives of millions are judged by Him according to what they had, and not according to what they had not, the nation of which they are units is an object of deep interest to Him, and He is leading it, according to principles of infallible wisdom, into its day of light and liberty. That day for India appears now to be at hand; and if we cannot understand all the purposes of God in the events of her past history, we have light enough in her early dawning to read a part of His meaning, and we must have faith to trust Him for the rest. We can at least see cause for thankfulness in the order in which God has allowed Popery and Christian truth to try their powers upon the idolatries of India. Was there not mercy in the arrangements that 'that should not be first which was spiritual, but that which was natural, and afterwards that which was spiritual;' in allowing Romanism to manifest its moral impotence when there was no other agent at work to lend it reputation, or to divide its shame, and then bringing in the simple but powerful Gospel among a people who, wherever the Romish priest had trod, would be warned by the worthlessness of Romanism against a mere change of names and ceremonies, and taught, by the contrast of what is real with what is nominal, that there is a Christianity which consists in a living faith in the Saviour, and spiritual worship of the Spirit God.

BY J. F. B. TINLING, B.A.

THE FOUNTAIN FOR SIN, AND OTHER AD-DRESSES. Price 6d.

AN EVANGELIST'S TOUR ROUND INDIA. Price 1s. 6d.

AN ECHO OF THE VOICE OF GEORGE FOX. A Letter to the Society of Friends. Price 4d.

BY MISS HETTY BOWMAN.

THOUGHTS FOR WORKERS AND SUFFERERS. Second Edition. Elegantly bound. Price 1s. 6d.

STUDIES IN THE PSALMS. Elegantly bound. Price 2s.

SONGS AMID THE SHADOWS. Price 1s.

LEAFLETS FOR LETTERS :—"Guidance," "The Church in Danger," "The Master's Voice" and "The Battle fought and won." Price 3d. per dozen; "Not Alone," Price 1½d. per dozen.

Price Two Shillings and Sixpence.

HISTORY OF THE TEMPORAL POWER OF THE POPES.

Showing the Crimes by which it was originally acquired, and afterwards enlarged.

BY W. ELFE TAYLER.

A Book for Aged People in large type.

JUST PUBLISHED, PRICE 2s.

FAITH'S PROVINCE & PRIVILEGE TO LOOK UP

From the World, and Sin, and Satan, unto Him who is "Mighty to Save," and "Able to do exceeding abundantly above all we ask or think."

BY DAVID A. DOUDNEY, D.D.,

Vicar of St. Luke's, Bedminster, Bristol.

THE IN MEMORIAM ALBUM.

In this Book a recognised want is met. Memorial Cards, now so generally issued on the death of beloved relatives and valued friends, after lying upon our tables for a few days, are put away or lost for the want of a proper repository, which it is confidently hoped the present Album will supply.

CLOTH, GILT EDGES, WITH LINEN GUARDS, TO HOLD 36 CARDS. .. 7s. 6d.
FRENCH MOROCCO, DO. DO. CLASP „ 48 „ .. 13 6
MOROCCO, DO. DO. DO. „ 48 „ .. 17 6

Bristol : W. Mack, 38, Park Street.

BY MR. GEORGE MÜLLER,

Of the Orphan Houses, Bristol.

FUNERAL SERMON of the late Mrs. GEORGE MÜLLER, of Bristol. Price 2d.

SATISFIED WITH GOD. Delivered shortly after the death, and at the funeral of Mrs. MÜLLER. Price 1d.

THE SECRET OF EFFECTUAL SERVICE TO GOD. Enamelled covers, 1d.

(An Edition of this Address on tinted paper, printed in a small size for postal circulation, 6d. per dozen).

LOVE ONE ANOTHER. The substance of two Addresses to Christians. Enamelled covers, 1d.

(An Edition on tinted paper, printed in a small size for postal circulation, 6d. per dozen).

CHILDREN OF GOD BY FAITH IN CHRIST JESUS. Enamelled covers, 1d.

(An Edition on tinted paper, printed in a small size for postal circulation, 6d. per dozen.)

THE GOSPEL IN THE HOLY GHOST. The substance of an Address to Christians.

> "Our Gospel came not unto you in word only, but also in power, and in the Holy Ghost, and in much assurance."— I THESS. i. 5.

(Printed in a small size for postal circulation, 6d. per dozen.)

A FEW WORDS ON "CRUCIFIED, DEAD, AND RISEN WITH JESUS." Enamelled covers, 1d; 13 copies for 1s.

(An Edition of this Address can also be had at 6d. per dozen, or 3s. 6d. per 100.)

THE WORD SENT AND THE WORD WRITTEN. AND THE SERVICE OF THE FATHER IN THE SPIRIT OF THE SON. The Substance of Two Addresses. Price 1d.

HOW TO PROMOTE THE GLORY OF GOD. An Address at a United Meeting for Prayer. Price 1d.

WALKING BY FAITH, NOT BY SIGHT. AND JEALOUSY FOR GOD IN A GODLESS WORLD. The substance of two Addresses. Price 1d.

THE MIGHTY GOD, AND WAITING FOR HIM. Two Addresses delivered at a United Meeting for Prayer. Price 1d.

LEANING UPON THE BELOVED. Price 6d. per doz.

Bristol: W. Mack, 38, Park Street.

BY REV. DR. DOUDNEY,

Incumbent of St. Luke's, Bedminster. (Editor of "Old Jonathan" and "Gospel Magazine.")

SERVICE AT HOME FOR THE YOUNG FOLKS IN SCHOOLS AND FAMILIES, for wet Sundays and Winter evenings. Post 8vo, neat cloth, 3s.

"OLD JONATHAN'S" HYMN-BOOK, for the use of Schools and Families. Intended as a companion for " Service at Home on Wet Sundays and Winter Evenings." Price 2d.

BIBLE LIVES AND BIBLE LESSONS; OR, GLEANINGS FROM THE BOOK OF GENESIS. Crown 8vo, price 3s.

WORDS FOR WEARY ONES; OR WHY WEEPEST THOU? Crown 8vo. Second Edition. Price 1s. 6d.

TRY, AND TRY AGAIN. By OLD JONATHAN. A Book for Boys. Ninth Thousand. With numerous Illustrations, and beautiful full-page Photographic Frontispiece. Price 3s. 6d.

LIGHT ON SCRIPTURE IN DAILY WALKS. Price 3d.

HAPPY JOHN, THE DYING POLICEMAN. With a Frontispiece of the House where he died, and the Cemetery where he was buried. Price 1d, or 7s. per 100; larger edition 2d. each, or 12s per 100.

THE POWER OF THE GOSPEL, as witnessed beside the dying-beds of Christians, in contrast to the ends of Romanists and Rationalists. Price 6d.

HEART BREATHINGS. Price 1s. 6d.

LEAVES FROM MY NOTE BOOK. Price 1s. 6d.

PILGRIM PAPERS, OR, COUNSEL, COMFORT, AND CAUTION FOR CHRISTIAN TRAVELLERS. Price 1s. 6d.

THE POWER & PRECIOUSNESS OF SAVING FAITH. Price 3d.

THE PUBLICAN'S CURIOSITY. A Sermon. Price 1d.

CARTE-DE-VISITE OF REV. DR. DOUDNEY. Price 1s.

"YET:" A Motto for all Times and Seasons. Being a Selection of Texts, in which God's Promises and Faith's Plea are most encouragingly presented. Price 2s.

Bristol: W. Mack, 38, Park Street.